VOLUME 3

Edited by **Jeff Conner**

Illustrated by **Mike Dubisch**

Cover painting by **Menton3**

SAN DIEGO, CA
2011

Book Design by Robbie Robbins

www.IDWPUBLISHING.com

ISBN: 978-1-60010-964-5

14 13 12 11   1 2 3 4

Become our fan on Facebook **facebook.com/idwpublishing** • Follow us on Twitter **@idwpublishing** • Check us out on YouTube **youtube.com/idwpublishing**

Ted Adams, CEO & Publisher • Greg Goldstein, Chief Operating Officer • Robbie Robbins, EVP/Sr. Graphic Artist
Chris Ryall, Chief Creative Officer/Editor-in-Chief • Matthew Ruzicka, CPA, Chief Financial Officer • Alan Payne, VP of Sales

REQUIRED READING REMIX, VOLUME 3. JUNE 2011. FIRST PRINTING. Required Reading Remix © 2011 Idea and Design Works, LLC. All Rights Reserved. Cover painting copyright © 2011 by Menton J. Mathews III. Illustrations copyright © 2011 by Mike Dubisch. All stories copyright © 2011 by their respective authors. IDW Publishing, a division of Idea and Design Works, LLC. Editorial offices: 5080 Santa Fe St., San Diego, CA 92109. Any similarities to persons living or dead are purely coincidental. With the exception of artwork and/or brief text excerpts used for review purposes, none of the contents of this publication may be reprinted without the permission of Idea and Design Works, LLC. Printed in Korea.
IDW Publishing does not read or accept unsolicited submissions of ideas, stories, or artwork.
Originally published as part of *Classics Mutilated*.

Table of Contents

꧁ ꧂

REQUIRED READING
READING
REMIXED

Anne-droid of Green Gables

By

Lezli Robyn

The Station Master whistled to himself while the steam engine puffed into the small Bright River station, rocking back and forth on the balls of his feet as he checked his brass pocket watch to verify the arrival time for his logbook. He had been told to expect an important delivery today, and so he was personally going to oversee the unloading of the cargo carriage. There wasn't much excitement to be had on Prince Edward's Island, so he was very curious as to what the package contained; he'd been told to unpack the box with care upon arrival.

The train chugged slowly to a stop, and the Station Master scanned the carriages to see if all was in order before pressing an ornate but bulky button on his lapel pocket. It whirred perceptively and then emitted a piercing whistle to alert the passengers that the train was safe to disembark.

He tilted his hat in greeting to the first young lady to step onto the platform, but she didn't have eyes for him. She was gazing about her with a soft smile on her face, smoothing out her skirts. So he made his way to the back of the train, signaling for Oswald to keep watch on the platform while he began to search for the precious cargo, and wondering why the owner hadn't arrived yet.

On the way he detoured to pull a brass lever on the side of a machine fixed to the platform near the last carriage door. The device wheezed to life, numerous brass and wooden cogs beginning to whirl around, steam pumping out of several exhaust valves as the leather conveyer belt sluggishly sprung into action. He then walked into the carriage and lit the gas lamp hanging just inside the doorway, automatically picking up and placing all the small packages and bags onto the conveyer belt so they would be transferred to the station office for sorting.

He paused when he came across a large trunk in the dark recesses of the carriage, the layer of dust that shrouded it a testament to its long journey on more trains than this one. He grabbed the lantern and held it over the trunk, wiping the corner clean to expose the sender's stamp.

"LUMIERE'S REFURBISHED MACHINES-TO-GO"

Satisfied, the Station Master pulled out his Universal Postal Service key and inserted the etched brass device into the leather buckle locks that were holding the lid of the trunk down. He heard a perceptible whir as the key activated in each lock, and they sprung open. He paused, his hand hovering just above the lid, wondering what he would find in the trunk. It was not often that city machines, even refurbished ones, made their way to the tiny coastal towns.

His curiosity got the better of him. The stamp told him that the trunk would be too heavy to carry off the carriage without extra help, so he knelt down, checked that all of the buckles had completely disengaged, and lifted the lid slowly.

Only to find himself looking into a pair of brilliant green eyes.

They blinked and then focused on him.

His blinked too, very rapidly, his mind a jumble of uncoordinated thoughts.

A small hand reached out of the trunk and took the lid from the Station Master's frozen grasp, pushing it completely open.

The man's mouth fell agape in response, as he stared anew at the trunk in wonder. Matthew Cuthbert had always been a man of few words, but his reticence in this case was a little extreme. A machine indeed!

There, pulling itself into sitting position, was an *android*. The Station Master had never seen one of those sophisticated machines before, and he didn't know how to go about interacting with them.

"Are you my new Father?" the android asked.

He shook his head somewhat absently, gathered his wits together, and rediscovered his voice. "Your new owner will be here soon," he offered gruffly. He gestured towards the carriage doorway. "Shall we go wait for him?"

The android looked towards the doorway and then back to him. "I can go *outside*?"

Again, he was taken aback. "Of course. If you want to meet your new owner you *have* to."

He stood up and hesitated, looking down at the android sitting in the battered travel trunk, and then reached down. A dainty hand rose to meet his, and he was startled by its warmth. For some reason he had expected android skin to be cold. Lifeless.

Like a machine.

But, instead, the hand he clasped in his own felt like that of a child. Somehow that thought put his mind at ease. He helped the android out of the trunk and then stepped out of the carriage, turning back to see what such an advanced machine would make of their humble station.

The android moved tentatively into the light and the Station Master gasped. It was female in form! He had previously thought all androids were made to appear androgynous.

He watched her look up in wonder at the sun when she felt its rays fall upon her face. In the full sunlight her skin shimmered with a slightly golden hue, but that was not her most distinguishing feature. It was her hair—or more the point, her two braids of very thick, decidedly red, woven copper filaments that fell down her back. The worn sailor hat didn't disguise the brilliance of the fine metallic strands, nor did the yellowed threadbare dress detract from the elegance of her form. While too slender to be considered very feminine, and her face too angular to ever be considered classically beautiful, she was a striking figure with her huge expressive eyes and the delicate brass nails that graced her little fingers.

In one hand the android held a carpet bag that had clearly seen better days, but she was holding it with such care that the Station Master couldn't help but be intrigued. He'd never considered the fact that an android could have luggage; it must have been stowed in the trunk with her.

She moved forward, turning around slowly as if to soak everything in, but when she spotted the conveyer belt she walked up to it, curious, and without preamble started fiddling with the various levers and cogs on the side with her free hand, only flinching—but not pulling back—when the steam from one valve hit her.

She had clearly done this before. Her tiny hand fit into the tight spaces to tweak this or that with such precision that within minutes the machine was running smoother, much to the Station Master's astonishment. She kept working until the chugging sound of the machine had turned into a soft purr, and then she turned back to the Station Master, who stammered his thanks.

"Oh, no need to thank me," she replied. "This machine is a primitive version of the sorting machines I used to operate at my previous home every day. It's such a pleasure to be able to work out how things operate, don't you think?" The android didn't give him the time to answer. "I've always thought so. There is something beautiful about seeing a machine work to the optimum of its capacity."

The Station Master couldn't agree more. He couldn't take his eyes off the android in front of him. She was an absolute marvel. He wondered where her new owner was.

He turned slightly and gestured towards the station building. "Would you like to wait in the Ladies Sitting Room until Mr. Cuthbert arrives?"

She tilted her head, considering both him and his offer. "No thank you," she replied. "I'll wait outside. There's more scope for the imagination."

The Station Master smiled. What a charming girl.

Matthew Cuthbert looked at the android from the far end of the platform and hesitated. He had never been much of a conversationalist, and had always found talking to girls to be one of the most awkward experiences in the world, so it was daunting for him to discover his most recent purchase was female in form. He had been told that he was buying a prototype whose model had never been put on the production line, but he hadn't thought to ask about gender.

He couldn't help but be intrigued, however, despite his anxiety. Androids had first been created to replace the child workforce in the factories that were expanding throughout the major cities. For many years children had often been the cheapest and most practical workers because their tiny hands and slight forms meant that they were able to manipulate delicate machinery, and so naturally the androids were modeled after them. But their creators soon discovered that their clientele did not want their new workforce looking like children—innocents. Nor did they like that the prototypes were created with advanced problem-solving skills, because some people believed it gave the androids individuality as they adapted to what they learnt, leading them to want to try new things outside the factory walls. As a consequence, the androids that eventually populated the factories all over Canada were created to be completely unremarkable in their subservience and androgynous appearance.

Matthew couldn't fathom how they could be considered superior in design to the original prototypes, but he wasn't going to complain. It meant he could afford to buy the "flawed" machine sitting on the platform in front of him.

He took a deep breath and walked towards the android—and then right on past. He realized at the last moment that he had no idea what to say to her. *How exactly does one greet an android?*

He reached the end of the platform, and stood there for a minute before turning around to see the android now eying him with evident curiosity. Matthew wondered what such a sophisticated machine would make of him, for he was very unassuming in appearance. Tall, with lank shoulder-length hair that was now more steel-colored than the black of his youth, he had a stooped frame, as if his very posture reflected his wish to not stand out in a crowd. But the shy smile he gave the android when he finally walked up to her was welcoming, and his eyes were kind. Before he even had time to consider how to greet her, the android had stood up and reached out her hand.

"You must be my new father, Matthew Cuthbert of Green Gables." She shook his hand in greeting, still clutching the carpet bag to her side. "I'm Anne—Anne with an *e*. Most people believe that Anne is short for *android*, and so often they leave off the *e* when they write it down. However the *e* is the letter that completes the name. If I met someone else called Anne, but spelt without the *e*, I just couldn't help but feel they were somehow lacking. What do you think, Mr. Cuthbert?"

He blinked, surprised. "Well, now, I dunno." He had a simple intelligence, but he wondered if the android was expressing her insecurities about being accepted. And more important, did she *know* she was doing that? "Can I take your bag?"

"No thank you, Mr. Cuthbert. I can manage. I have to make sure I hold the handle with a 43-degree tilt at all times or it's prone to falling off. An extra degree either way and the bag has an 82 percent chance of losing its structural integrity. It's a very old, very dear carpet bag."

Matthew smiled at the unexpected mix of technical evaluation and human sentiment in Anne's statement, seemingly fitting for a machine made in Man's image. He gestured for the android to follow him, and they made their way to his horse and buggy in silence, Matthew looking at the ground, and Anne looking at everything else.

She appeared captivated by the most commonplace things. Even while one of the very rare and expensive steam-operated carriages rolled on by with the girl from the train gracing its leather seat, protecting her fair skin with her lace parasol, Anne's attention stayed focused on the old draft horse hitched to Matthew's buggy.

"I'm at a loss to see how you power this locomotive," she replied after a moment.

The corner of Matthew's mouth twitched, and he ducked his head to hide a smile, realizing that the android had never seen a horse before, and that this particular one was close to comatose.

He walked up to the horse, rubbing the gelding's neck gently, prompting him to shake out his mane and seemingly coming to life. "There are no steam-generated levers needed to operate this buggy. I just tell Samuel here to pull it for me."

The android blinked. "Samuel isn't a machine?"

"No," he said simply.

"But this creature's purpose is to serve humans?" she asked, her head tilting to the side.

Matthew's hand paused mid-stroke. "Well, yes, I suppose in a way that's true."

"Does it have free will?"

This time it was Matthew who blinked. "He lives and works on my farm."

She didn't miss a beat. "Because he has no other choice."

"Yes."

She nodded to herself. "I understand."

Matthew was struck by how definitive her answer was. "How so?"

"That existence was not unlike my life at the factory." She reached out her hand and gingerly mimicked Matthew's actions a minute earlier, her brass nails glinting in the filtered sunlight as she rubbed the horse's neck.

Matthew watched her for a long moment, then: "Did that bother you? Being told what to do all the time, I mean."

"No. Why would it?"

Matthew didn't know how to reply.

Anne continued on, almost absently. "I like to learn, and to keep busy. I also like to discover how things work. The Supervisor told me that that was a flaw in my make-up, and that I had to be terminated. I didn't know why I was going to lose my job when I had just surprised him by halting production of the main sorting machine in the factory to improve its performance by 6.3 percent, but he wouldn't listen to me anymore." Her hand stilled, and the horse head-butted her to resume. "It was Father who intervened. He told the Supervisor that termination was too final a punishment, and that I could still be of some use. However, I don't understand what he meant by that comment, because I no longer work for the company."

Matthew's depleted bank balance told him exactly how Anne had still been of use to the company, but it was her naiveté that fascinated him the most, not the reason why she had been sold.

The journey home was filled with more discoveries for them both, the android talking non-stop and the man appreciating the fact that she didn't expect him to talk too.

"You and I are going to get along just fine, Mr. Cuthbert."

"Call me Matthew."

"I'm not sure why I know this, or why I know I belong at Green Gables, but I've always thought there was more...."

The android stopped mid-sentence, her crystal green eyes going wide as her eyes fixed on the sky in front of her. For a moment Matthew couldn't take his eyes away from Anne's face, struck by how the sense of wonder really bought her features to life. But her attention didn't waver, so he drew his gaze away from her striking features to look up and see an airship sailing gently through the sky, the golden light of the setting sun lapping against the hull as it gently surfed the clouds.

It was barely perceptible to Matthew, but he was sure that Anne could hear the whir of the enormous steam engine at work, pumping hot air into an enormous canvas balloon that the old seafaring ship was now suspended from.

"What a wondrous invention!" the android breathed in amazement.

Matthew looked back at her in surprise. "How so?"

She turned to him with bright eyes. "This machine gives you the ability to fly, which would be one of the most incredible experiences. Imagine being able to look down at the world! It would create such a sense of freedom, don't you think?"

He nodded. He'd never thought of it that way before.

"Have you ever considered flying in one of those machines?"

"No, I can't say as I have," he replied, intrigued by her child-like curiosity.

"Oh, Matthew, how much you miss out on!" They both looked back up at the airship in shared silence for a long minute.

Matthew glanced at Anne out of the corner of his eye, amazed that such a so-phisticated machine could be in such awe of an old seafaring ship that had clearly seen better days. It had been hobbled to a simple canvas balloon and operated by the most cumbersome steam engine he had ever encountered, simply so its owner could maximize his resources and try to keep at the cutting edge of the transport industry. He supposed the idea was ingenious, but the execution didn't strike him as being very safe or too elegant.

"I have worked with many machines," the android said quietly, her gaze still on the airship as it disappeared slowly over the horizon, "but I have never seen one that was so beautiful."

"I have," Matthew responded in his quiet, shy manner. "*You.*"

She turned to him, her eyes now wide. "But I'm just a girl."

The innocence in her statement went straight to his heart. Matthew had never been one to talk much, but now he was literally speechless.

She didn't see herself as a machine!

Although he didn't realize it at the time, that was the moment *he* stopped seeing her as one too.

Anne discovered that being accepted by her classmates at school wasn't something she could learn from an instruction manual. When she queried Matthew about how to secure a Bosom Friend, he simply told her to "Be yourself," which puzzled her as she couldn't physically be anyone other than herself anyway. When she asked his wife the same question, however, her curt response was "Forget that nonsense! If you prove your worth, friendships will seek you out. Be kind, considerate, and above all, bite that tongue and mind your manners!"

"Biting my tongue will help facilitate friendships?" Anne asked, perplexed.

"You do beat all, girl! Of course not," Marilla replied, frustrated. "It's an expression—a human expression. But then, I suppose you shouldn't be expected to know that."

The old lady sighed, looking at the android. Ever since Matthew had bought Anne home, the peace and order at Green Gables had been thrown into disarray.

"We have to send her back," she had told him the very first hour he'd returned home with the android.

"But she's such a sweet little thing," he had replied softly as he watched Anne walk around the house for the first time, reaching out her hand to touch the most random of things in fascination: the intricate embroidery on the tablecloth, the leaves of a plant, or the polished wood of the rocking chair. She had never seen such diverse textures before.

"Matthew Cuthbert, the entire reason for buying an android in the first place was so you can have help on the farm. It's unseemly to put a girl to work in the fields, even if she is android in form. And we're both too old to be nursemaids to a flawed machine."

"She's not flawed—just different." Matthew paused. "Give her a chance, Marilla."

"We'd have to put her through school, simply so she can learn the basics of interacting in society."

"So she'll go to school."

"But what is the point of buying an android if we can't get our money's worth out of her? There is still the matter of you needing help on the farm."

"I'll hire Barry's boy out for a couple of hours during the day, and Anne can help me before and after school." He held up his hand to forestall Marilla's next protest. "We can't afford to buy a normal android. And the simple fact is: I like her." He looked at his wife. "I don't ask for much, but I'm asking for this."

Marilla harrumphed, more to cover her shock than out of any deep need to protest. This was the first time her husband had ever stood up to her and held his ground. This machine must have really gotten under his skin. "The android can stay," she stated finally, "but strictly on a trial basis. We have a three-month warranty, don't we?"

"Yes."

"Then if I'm not impressed by that time, we are returning her for a full refund. And I want no protests, Matthew. That is my condition for letting her stay now."

Matthew nodded, satisfied. He knew that despite the condition, he'd just won a great concession from his wife.

And so every morning Matthew came downstairs to the library at five to find Anne engrossed in one of his books, looking more like the child she appeared to be as she acted out the plays with enthusiasm, the dying light of the fire dancing about in her copper hair. They would talk about her latest literary discoveries of the previous night while Matthew ate his breakfast, and then their day would start, the android helping Matthew milk the cows, muck out the stables, and carry out all the hay for the animals until it was time for her to leave for school.

Within a week they had developed a comfortable routine, and Matthew was surprised to discover that for the first time in a decade he actually enjoyed getting up before the birds awoke. However, it soon became clear after a few weeks of school that Anne hadn't been able to make as favorable an impression on her classmates, who were quick to point out how different she was.

"People don't often like that which they don't understand," Marilla had told the android matter-of-factly.

But Anne had read about "kindred spirits" and how true bosom friends are accepting of all differences, and as Marilla had said, she just had to prove she was worthy of being a perfect friend.

So every day she went to school and tried to prove herself by excelling in her classwork. She had much to learn, having only known factory life before Green Gables, but it didn't take long until she was tied with Gilbert Blythe for first honors.

And still the classmates' attitude towards her didn't noticeably thaw. The android couldn't understand why. Wasn't she doing everything right?

"You think you are better than us, don't you, Miss Anne-*droid*?" was Josie Pye's snide comment after Anne won her first spelling bee. She twisted around at her desk to look directly at Anne. "Can you spell *machine?*"

Anne looked at her in puzzlement. *Is this another test?* "M-A-C-H-I—"

"Do you always have an answer for *everything?*" Josie interrupted, frustrated that she could never get a rise out of the copper-haired girl.

"Isn't the correct response to a question an answer?" she asked, still puzzled.

Josie glared at her and faced forward again, not speaking to her until their extracurricular painting class that evening. "I'm sure you are perfect at that too," she muttered.

"I don't know," the android replied. "I've never painted before."

The class set up outside to capture the majesty of the rolling fields of Avonlea on canvas. Nestled in the tree line along the horizon, Anne could see the roof of Green Gables, and so she painted that first, her strokes precise and her measurements exact.

Then she moved to the fields, taking care to note the exact hue of the grass and blending the appropriate golden-hued green. Within fifteen minutes the field was done, complete with fences drawn to scale.

While Anne was busy duplicating the trees on her canvas, the teacher went up to each student in turn to ascertain their progress and study what their diverse depictions of the one view told him about their personalities.

When he approached Anne, his eyebrows raised at the quality of the painting. Then they furrowed. "Well, it's technically perfect," he said, and he sat down to start his painting.

Diana Berry looked up from her canvas as Anne was starting to outline the clouds. The raven-haired beauty glanced at Anne's painting, her blue eyes going wide. "Oh Anne! I wish I could paint half as good as you do!"

"Honey, you don't need to be talented with looks like yours," Gilbert Blythe quipped from somewhere behind them. The other students snickered and the light disappeared out of Diana's eyes. She returned them to her painting.

Anne looked up from her masterpiece to discover the clouds had moved. Quickly she started painting their new position over the clouds she had already started to form.

Then she noticed that the sun had changed position. Its lower angle threw a deeper amber cast onto the field. Frantically she started to mix up a different shade of green to replace the grass she'd painted earlier.

Then she noticed that the new position of the sun meant that Green Gables was completely in shadow, rendering the cottage almost invisible to the naked eye. So Anne painstakingly painted it into a silhouette.

Then she looked up to see salmon pink was starting to outline the bottom of the clouds, and a peach was spreading across the horizon. The sun was setting.

Her efforts to keep up with the changing colors of encroaching night meant her painting strokes increased to inhuman speed—and she *still* couldn't keep up. Every time she looked up, her painting was no longer accurate. The trees were now completely black along the horizon, and the fences cast long shadows across the field.

She stopped, at a loss for what to do. As a result of changing the colors in the sky so often and so quickly in a blur of hand and brush, the layers didn't have enough time to dry, resulting in the salmon pink blending with the earlier lighter blue shades. Her sky was now a mauve color. It was a restful shade, throwing a slightly romantic mood over the painting, but all Anne could see was that it wasn't an accurate depiction.

Josie snickered. "It looks like Anne can't do everything right after all."

"Don't listen to her," Diana said, a little pointedly. "Josie doesn't think of anyone but herself." She looked at Anne's painting. "Why did you keep changing the colors? Not that it looks bad," she added hastily, "but your painting looked perfectly fine before."

"The colors are all wrong."

Gilbert appeared over her shoulder, his usual nonchalant stance dissipating in his interest. "In what way?" he asked.

"We were told to paint this view." Anne gestured in front of her. "But the colors keep changing. This painting is no longer accurate."

"A painting doesn't have to be technically accurate for it to be considered a masterpiece," the teacher interjected, only his blond hair visible at the top of his canvas as he continued to paint. "It's how you interpret the view that brings the painting to life."

"I don't understand," said Anne.

"Take a look at mine," Diana offered, a little shyly.

Anne stood up and walked over, studying the painting for a long moment. "The clouds are the wrong shape."

"Not the *wrong* shape, Anne. Just a *different* shape," she replied. "It's a matter of perspective. Take a closer look."

The android tilted her head to the side, as she always did when she was thinking, and considered the clouds Diana had painted. They were perhaps a little too white. Also the strokes she used to define the texture of the clouds were too coarse to depict the lightness of the gossamer structures.

"Pretend they aren't clouds," Gilbert interrupted her thoughts. "What else do you see?"

Anne considered the shapes of the clouds and nothing else, and automatically started comparing them to images in her memory banks. "They're animals!" she blurted out suddenly, Diana laughing as the android's eyes darted up to the sky. Sure enough, she could see the remnants of some of the clouds Diana had painted. If she looked closely enough, she could see what looked like a rabbit bounding over the horizon. "How did you know to do this?" she asked finally.

"I just used my imagination," Diana replied, blushing delicately at the attention.

"But androids don't have an imagination, do they, Gilbert?" Josie pointed out, twirling her hair around her finger.

"Knock it off, Josie." Gilbert replied. "Nobody's perfect. She just had to know how to look."

Anne didn't hear them. She was still trying to process what she had just learned. "So Diana's painting is better than mine, even though mine is technically more accurate."

The teacher leaned around his easel. "*Better* is not the right word. It's a more *realized* painting." He paused, trying to work out how to explain it. "Your painting shows us how you—or anyone here—physically sees the fields, but nothing more. It doesn't show us anything about *you*."

She analyzed his words carefully, and found herself, as well as her painting, lacking. "So I have failed."

"No, not necessarily." The teacher studied the android for a moment, aware that she'd probably never been confronted with failure before.

"It just means you've got more to learn." He smiled gently. "That is what school is for."

"Where do I start?"

Even Josie was struck by the earnest entreaty in the android's tone.

"Here and now," the teacher responded with a smile. "We've still got a half an hour of light."

The android sat down at her easel, unwilling to let the teacher know he had misunderstood her. She remembered what happened when the Supervisor at the factory had misunderstood her, and she didn't want to be sold again. She looked at her painting.

Where do I start?

"Do you see Green Gables in the distance?" Diana whispered into Anne's ear, leaning over in her chair. Anne nodded. "That is not merely where you live, but it's your *home*. What do you *see* when you think of home?"

Diana watched Anne's eyes blink rapidly for a few seconds, and then flitter back and forth across the painting. She reached for her paints and brush, and started mixing colors.

Diana watched, fascinated, while Anne started applying paint to the canvas once more. Her speed belied her android heritage as an airship quickly took shape amongst the clouds in the painting's mauve sky.

When the flying vessel was complete, she dipped her brush in a combination of pots and leaned forward. For a minute Diana could only see the back of Anne's copper braid as the android painstakingly painted a candlelit window onto the silhouette of the cottage, but then she leaned back and dipped her brush into black pot.

After considering the painting for a moment, the android started to paint a tiny profile of a human in the field closest to the cottage. When she also brushed in a little cattle dog beside the figure, Diana realized that it was Anne's depiction of Matthew returning to Green Gables after a hard day's work on the farm.

The android's hand hesitated beside the image of the man, and Diana wondered if the android understood what a lovely—and homely—image she had just created: the light from the kitchen guiding the man home at night.

But then the android's hand darted upwards, and another silhouette started to take shape at the bow of the airship. It appeared that the figure was looking down at the cottage, and when Diana saw that the silhouette wore her hair in a braid that was lifted by the wind, Diana started in shock.

Anne had drawn herself into the painting, and she was sailing on an airship, being guided home by the cottage light like a seafaring ship would a lighthouse.

Who said androids couldn't have an imagination? Diana thought triumphantly, looking at her new friend's painting with a smile on her face. *Anne might be a kindred spirit after all.*

Matthew pulled out his timepiece and opened the case to see where the clock hands pointed. "It's time to leave for school, Anne," he said quietly, sure that she could hear him from across the barn.

She looked up, blinking in surprise. "Usually my internal clock alerts me before now."

Matthew nodded, bemused. One of the things that endeared him the most about the android was that she could often get so swept up in her enthusiasm and curiosity for the current project she was working on that it overrode her most basic mechanical functions, like her inbuilt alarm clock. He knew that Marilla and Anne's creators considered that a manufacturing flaw, but to Matthew it seemed like a very human characteristic.

He watched her methodically put his tools back in order, and then cover the machine.

"I was nearly finished!" she complained.

"So you will finish it tonight."

"I suppose that is an acceptable conclusion," she replied.

Matthew laughed. *Was the android pouting?* "Well, my dear Anne, if this contraption of yours truly works and I never have to milk a cow again with my bare hands, then I will have the time to start teaching you chess before school tomorrow morning." He smiled at her. "Is that also an acceptable conclusion?"

It appeared to him that her eyes lit up. "More than acceptable, Matthew." She tilted her head, considering him.

Matthew blushed under her scrutiny and busied himself with closing his time-piece and running his thumb lovingly over the initials ornately carved across the lid before moving to put it away. He felt the android's curiosity before she voiced it. "It was my father's," he said quietly. He hesitated a moment, then held it out to her.

Anne appeared to understand the privilege she was being given. She took the pocket watch from Matthew with evident care, turning it around in her dainty hands to look at the initials, almost imperceptible on the old tarnished metal. She popped the lid open, and her eyes grew wide. She had never seen such a tiny machine. Behind the ornately carved brass hands, she could see the intricate wheels turn, and despite the discoloration of age, she thought it beautiful.

Matthew let the android hold his timepiece the entire way to school, the light reflecting off Anne's brass nails as she tinkered with it, drawing his attention to the advancement of her construction in comparison to his beloved pocket watch. The 19th century had seen a huge evolution in machines, and he wondered what the next century would bring if Anne was the pinnacle of this one.

The buggy started rocking more than usual, with Samuel having to navigate more ruts as a result of the storm the previous night, but when Matthew briefly glanced over at Anne he saw the pocket watch clutched protectively in her tiny hand.

She seemed almost reluctant to give it up when they reached the school, but then she heard Diana calling and she quickly handed it over, leaping out of the buggy with her usual enthusiasm and grace. She turned to Matthew to say good-bye, and he told her he'd be there at three to pick her up.

"No need, Matthew," she said. "Gilbert Blythe said he'd walk me to the bend, and I wanted to see the new flowers that have come out since the last rain."

Matthew smiled as he watched her rush off to greet Diana, wondering if she realized how human she sounded.

He shook his head at his folly. *Of course she knows. She doesn't see herself as a machine!*

He laughed as Samuel pulled the buggy away from school, and he returned home with a smile still on his face.

"What time do you call this, Matthew Cuthbert?" Marilla asked when he walked into the kitchen to share a pot of tea with his wife before going back to work on the farm.

He didn't know why, but by Marilla's clock he was always late. He pulled out his pocket watch to check—and discovered it was no longer working.

His heart sank in his chest. His pocket watch had never failed him until today, and it was his last tangible memory of his father.

He looked at it closely and he could see that part of the clock mechanism appeared dislodged behind the face, and when he shook it gently, he could hear something metallic rattle around. It appeared that an irreplaceable component was broken in his beloved timepiece.

Marilla saw the look on his face and asked him what was wrong. After he told her, she asked, "What, if anything, did you do differently with the pocket watch today?"

He thought back on his morning. "Nothing, really. I gave it to Anne to look at, and then let her hold it while we travelled through some storm-created ruts on the way to school." He paused, considering. "Come to think of it, those ruts really were pretty rough going. I wouldn't be surprised if one of them was what did it."

Marilla wasn't convinced. "Did you watch Anne the entire time she had your timepiece, Matthew?"

"I can't say as I did," he replied, wondering what his wife was getting at. "I had to concentrate on the road on account of those bothersome ruts."

Marilla was silent for a long moment, and then she asked, "Do you think the android could have tinkered with it? She seems fascinated with the inner workings of machinery."

"Anne was fascinated by the intricacy of my pocket watch," he admitted. "But...."

"Think about it, Matthew," Marilla interrupted. "My theory makes sense. The pocket watch had never broken down in your lifetime, or your Dad's, *until* the day you let Anne play with it."

He couldn't find any fault with her logic, but deep down in his heart he knew it wasn't true.

When Anne came home that afternoon from her walk with Gilbert Blythe, a posy of wildflowers in her hand, Marilla confronted her. "Did you fiddle with the mechanism in Matthew's pocket watch?"

Anne noted the agitated tone in her voice, and became concerned. "What's wrong with it?"

Marilla took that as an admission of a kind. "So you *know* something is wrong with it!"

"No, Marilla," Anne replied. "I honestly didn't." She looked at Matthew, who was quietly sitting in the kitchen chair, watching the exchange. He gave her a gentle smile of encouragement.

"I need a truthful answer from you, Anne," said Marilla. "Did you play with Matthew's watch until you broke it?"

"No, Marilla," said Anne truthfully, since she had no idea when it broke.

"Then who did?" demanded Marilla.

Anne simply stared at her. She'd been taught never to guess when she didn't know the answer.

Marilla glared at the android, trying to keep her temper in check. "Now listen to me carefully, Anne," she said at last, ominously enunciating every syllable. "If you don't admit that you've done wrong, and that you just lied to me, you will not be allowed to go to Diana's birthday airship flight next month."

Anne's mind quickly considered the possibilities and the consequences. If she did not admit to purposely breaking the watch, Marilla would not believe her and she would not be permitted to ride on the exotic airship. On the other hand, if she lied and admitted to breaking it, Marilla almost certainly *would* believe her and she would be allowed to go. It was very confusing: if she lied she would be rewarded, and if she told the truth she would be punished.

Which was worse—to lie and be believed, or to tell the truth and be doubted? In the end it was not the airship that was the deciding factor, but a desire to please Marilla by telling her what Anne assumed she wanted to hear, and what she obviously already believed.

"I broke the watch while I was playing with it," she said at last.

Marilla stared at her a long time before speaking. Finally she said, "All right, Anne. Cuthberts always keep their word, so you will be allowed to go on the airship."

"Thank you," said Anne.

"I'm not finished yet," said Marilla harshly. "As I said, Cuthberts don't lie. You just admitted that you lied to me. Therefore, you are not and never will be a Cuthbert. I'm going to have a serious talk with Matthew after you're in bed tonight. I think we're going to return you and get our money back. You are *not* what we were promised."

Anne was still staring at the empty space where Marilla had stood long after Marilla had turned and walked away.

Deep down Anne had known she was different from everyone else in Avonlea, and that she had the means to repair the pocket watch if she only just acknowledged it. She didn't know if she had refused to accept the truth about herself and had blocked it from her mind, or if she had simply been programmed to not think about it, but she had to confront it now if she was to ever help fix the damage she had inadvertently caused.

She pulled out her carpet bag, and for the first time since she'd arrived at Green Gables she opened it up.

Inside was a batch of tools, some of them not unlike those she was using to create Matthew's milking machine, only finer in construction.

Her delicate hand reached in and sorted through them until she felt the one she needed and pulled it out, looking at it for a long moment.

She hesitated, then unlaced the top of her nightgown, looking down at the barely perceptible panel outlined on the left side of her chest. Her right hand hovered above it, implement in hand, knowing instinctively what she had to do, but unable to take the next step. Then she thought of the pain she saw in Matthew's eyes when Marilla had decreed she had to be returned to the factory, and she steeled herself, placing the implement along one side of the panel and pressing it in, hearing a tiny whir as three micro-latches started turning. A section of her popped out, and she looked at it for a long moment before carefully hooking the brass nail of her thumb into the tiny crevice and pulling it open.

I'm a machine.

The realization struck her like a punch to the stomach as she stood staring at what she had revealed, unable to process anything for some time. Although deep down she had always known, it was still a shock to see tiny brass cogs, wheels, screws, and copper wires so intricately interconnected to a circuit board buried within her chest. It was a wonder to behold, even for the android.

She realized how primitive the pocket watch was in comparison, and yet she also understood its importance to Matthew, and her determination to repair it for him increased tenfold. She closed her eyes and tuned into the sounds her body made.

Tick, tick, tick, tick...

Her eyes sprung open, and she instinctively moved a bundle of copper wires that were covering the specific mechanism she needed to find. She analyzed the individual components, recognizing that some were similar to those in the pocket watch.

Tick, tick, tick, tick...

She rustled around in her carpet bag and pulled out a tiny toolbox, opening it to reveal delicate jewellery-grade tools. She selected one and used it to sever the connection between the tiny mechanism and her main circuit board without a second thought.

The ticking stopped.

The android's hand froze. She felt a strong sense of loss, and she couldn't focus. She had no idea how long it took her to adjust to the change in her body, because she literally lost track of time, but she finally was able to block out the feeling that she had lost something fundamental to her being when she realized how much more she'd lose if she had to leave Green Gables.

She carefully placed the little mechanism on the table in front of her and used the firelight to study it more closely. At first she had thought she'd wasted her time, but when she put the pocket watch beside it, she was able to compare the components more easily, and she could see they were of similar composition and size; they were just finished off differently.

Then she spotted it: the part she needed.

Using the precision that only an android could command, Anne very carefully detached it and transplanted it into the pocket watch within minutes. When the last part was in place, the pocket watch sprang to life.

Tick, tick, tick, tick...

Anne clapped her hands together in delight, an affectation she'd picked up from Diana. She knew that what she achieved that night was more important than any work she'd ever done on the factory floor—or at least, it felt that way to her.

She looked at the part of herself she'd transplanted into the pocket watch, studying her handiwork, unable to find it lacking. The new part stood out from the rest of the components because it was free of tarnish and more rose gold in color than normal brass. It also appeared more refined in composition, and she wondered if Matthew would mind the discrepancy.

She resealed her access panel and relaced the top of her nightgown before methodically packing her tools back into the carpet bag. She considered whether she should clean the brass and restore the pocket watch back to its original condition. But the cleaning agent she normally rinsed through her copper hair was in the bathroom upstairs, and she didn't want to risk waking the Cuthberts.

She picked up the pocket watch again to take it back to the kitchen where Matthew had usually kept it, and walked straight into someone.

"Anne! Give that to me immediately!" Marilla barked, standing in the doorway with a lantern in her hand. "You have been told you are no longer welcome in our house, and that means you are definitely not allowed to touch our things." She looked at the android pointedly. "Especially ones you've already broken."

Anne didn't trust herself to speak after the trouble her mouth had gotten her into earlier that day, so instead she simply held out her hand.

Marilla was taken aback by the silent acquiesce. She looked down to see the pocket watch still open on the dainty little hand, and she wondered what other heirlooms the android had played with while she and Matthew had been asleep at night.

She retrieved the pocket watch, inspecting it to see if it came to further damage—and her heart nearly stopped.

The pocket watch was working again!

She couldn't tear her eyes away from it; she was so surprised. Then she spotted the gleaming new part at the heart of the clock mechanism, and her breath caught. "Where did you get that?" Marilla asked, looking up at Anne sharply.

The android raised her hand and placed it on her chest where a human heart would be. "Here," she said simply, her head tilting to the side.

She had used a part of herself to repair the watch! Marilla realized what a huge gesture that was. "You didn't break the watch yesterday by playing with the clock mechanism, did you?" she asked quietly.

"No."

Marilla sighed. "Then why did you say you did when I asked?"

"You told me I couldn't go on the airship for Diana's birthday celebration next month unless I confessed to breaking it," Anne said, her big green eyes seeking Marilla's out in entreaty. "So I confessed."

"But that's lying, Anne," Marilla pointed out.

"You wouldn't believe the truth."

Marilla sighed again. "So you thought you were giving me the answer I wanted. You were trying to please me." She looked back down at the repaired pocket watch. "Let us make a deal, Anne: I will forgive you for lying, if you will forgive me for not believing you."

"What is this about forgiveness?" Matthew asked, as he, too, walked into the room.

Marilla ate some humble pie. "You were right," she admitted, and without saying any more she handed over the pocket watch.

Matthew brought the timepiece closer to his lantern to study it. That it worked again was no surprise to him. He had a feeling Anne would try to repair it after watching her dedication while building his milking machine. But what he didn't expect to see was the glint of a new component in the clock mechanism that differed in color from the rest of the watch. He looked over to Anne in shock when he recognized its construction was far more refined than the rest of the watch's components.

Anne's green eyes twinkled. "I'll never be on time for school again," she said, and Matthew realized she'd used a component from her internal clock to bring his father's beloved pocket watch back to life.

He knew what a sacrifice that must have been for the android, and his heart reached out to her, knowing that in a way he held a piece of hers within in his hand.

He walked up to her and kissed her on the forehead, much to her and Marilla's surprise. "You'll just have to learn how to tell the time like us average folks," he said as he stepped back, his voice a little gruff with emotion.

"*I'll* teach you, Anne," Marilla stated. "If you learn from Matthew, you'll never arrive anywhere on time."

Anne had always thought that sailing on an airship would give her a sense of freedom unlike any other experience in the world.

She was wrong.

Yes, it was exhilarating. Yes, she felt on top of the world—quite literally—as she leaned over the bow of the ship, the wind lifting her copper hair as the vessel passed through another cloud bank. But she soon realized that she was just a spectator watching the world pass her by. There was some peace to be discovered in that, but she had no control over that journey; she just had to enjoy the ride.

She knew now that her first true taste of freedom had been when the Station Master had released her from the cargo trunk at the train station three months ago—she just hadn't been aware of it at the time. She had stepped out into a brand new world, with sensations she'd never even known had existed, let alone experienced, and for the first time in her brief life she had the opportunity to be accepted. Appreciated.

Loved.

No longer was she being told how to perform her every action like an automated machine. She had to learn and adapt to the ramifications of her actions like everyone else, and deal with any consequences that arose. There was a great sense of freedom in being in control of her own destiny that she'd previously been denied until she'd met the Cuthberts.

Her keen android eyes searched the fields far below her until she spotted Green Gables nestled along the treeline. As she gazed at it she felt a sense of belonging that she'd never experienced before.

"We would like to adopt you," Matthew said quietly when she had hopped off the airship not long after, halting her excited rambles about how the journey through the clouds had given her such scope for the imagination.

"But you have already bought me," Anne replied, perplexed, as she considered Matthew's shy smile.

"That's true," said Marilla, "and what an expensive girl you were, to say the least." She brushed off her skirts briskly, and then looked directly at the android, who returned her gaze. "But we don't want to *own* you," she added, reaching over to take hold of Matthew's hand. "We want to know if you would *choose* to become a part of this family as the child we never had, and never knew we'd even wanted until you came into our lives."

Anne stared at both of them, and for the first time since they met her, she was speechless.

In that moment she became Anne of Green Gables.

She had finally come home.

Little Women in Black

By

Louisa May Alcott and Rick Hautala

C hristmas won't be Christmas without any presents," grumbled Jo, sitting on the rug before the fire. She had a ball of yarn in her lap and, like her sisters, was busily knitting socks to send to the soldiers. Her hands moved somewhat clumsily because of the linen gloves she wore to cover up the scars, scabs, and open wounds on her hands. Even now, a few of them were bleeding through the thin fabric, making random blossoms of bright scarlet.

"It's so dreadful to be poor," sighed Meg, looking down with frustration at her old dress.

"It's not fair for some girls to have pretty things, and other girls nothing at all," added little Amy, with an injured sniff.

"We've still got Father and Mother … and each other," whispered Beth from her dark corner by the fireplace.

The three young faces on which the firelight shone brightened at the cheerful words so faint they could have been a thought in each one's mind, but their expressions darkened again when Meg said sadly, "But we *haven't* got Father … and the other dear one we lost and miss so much."

"We haven't lost Father," remarked Jo. "He's just away at the war."

"But we shan't have him for a very long time," added Amy, staring at the fire wistfully.

She didn't have to add the phrase "perhaps never," but each girl silently did as they paused to think of Father, far away down South. He was serving as a chaplain in Mr. Lincoln's Army, so he wouldn't see battle directly, but there were many other dangers of war he must face daily. How, each of them wondered, would all of that have changed him when he returned? How could it not help but change him from the kind, loving father they all knew and loved so much?

Nobody spoke for several minutes, the only sound the rhythmic clicking of knitting needles. Then Meg said, "You know the reason Mother proposed us not having any Christmas presents this year is because it is going to be a dreadfully hard winter for everyone, not just our troops. She thinks we ought not to spend any money for trinkets or silly pleasures when our soldiers are suffering so."

"We can't do much," added Jo, "but we can make little sacrifices and ought to do so gladly, I suppose." She paused, and then added sullenly, "But I'm afraid I don't do it gladly. I miss Father so."

Meg shook her head as she thought regretfully of all the pretty things she wanted and might never have.

"I don't think the little we would spend would do any good for the soldiers," said Amy. "We've each got a dollar, and the army wouldn't be much helped by our giving that away."

"I agree not to expect anything from Mother or you this season, but I so much want to buy Mr. Hawthorne's newest novel," Jo said.

"I had hoped to spend mine on some new sheet music," said Beth with a low, wistful sigh that no one heard but the hearth brush and kettle holder. Her pale face floated in the darkness like the moon, obscured by clouds, wavering and dimming. Meg cast a glance in Beth's direction and shivered as though she had caught a draft.

"Well, I shall get a nice new box of Faber's drawing pencils," declared Amy. "I really do need them."

"Mother didn't say anything about *our* money," cried Jo, "and she won't wish us to give up everything. Let us each buy what we want for ourselves and have a little fun. I'm sure we work hard enough to earn it."

"I know I certainly do, teaching those tiresome children all day when I'm longing to enjoy myself at home," said Meg.

"You don't have half such a hard time as I do," said Jo. "How would you like to be cooped up for hours on end with a fussy old lady like Aunt March, who keeps me trotting back and forth, is never satisfied, and worries me till I'm ready to fly out the window or break down and cry?"

"Don't fret," said Beth with a deep sigh that, when it ended, filled the room with a hush.

"I don't believe any of you suffer as I do," cried Amy, "for you don't have to go to school with impertinent girls who plague you if you don't know your lessons, and laugh at your simple dresses, and label your father as nothing but a poor minister."

"If you mean *libel*," said Jo, laughing, "I'd say so and not talk about *labels* as if Father were a pickle bottle."

"I say what I mean, and I mean what I say, and you needn't be satirical about it," said Amy, pouting with hurt dignity.

"Using that fine logic," said Meg, "you may as well say, 'I see what I eat, so I eat what I see.' "

"It's proper to use good words and improve your vocabulary," Amy replied with a huff.

"Don't peck at one another, children," said Meg, sounding more like Mother—their "Marmee"—than herself. "Don't you wish we had the money Father had when we were little, Jo? Dear me! How happy we were then, and how good we'd be now if we had no worries!"

"You said the other day that you thought we were a great deal happier than the Patterson children," Jo said, "for they are forever fighting and fretting in spite of their wealth."

"So I did." Beth said, shifting her gaze to the fire, sure she caught a gauzy flutter of motion in the darkest corner. "Well, I think we *are* happier, and all it will take to complete our happiness is for Father to return to us safely from the war. For though we do have to work, we are a jolly lot, all in all, as Jo would say."

"Jo does use such slang words," observed Amy, with a reproving look at the long figure now stretched on the rug. "At least I try to use a *vocabulary*."

Jo immediately sat up and, self-conscious of the scarlet splotches on her gloves, put her hands behind her back and began to whistle.

"Don't whistle like that, Jo. It's so … *boy*-ish," advised Meg. "It irritates me so."

"That's why I do it."

"Well I, for one, detest rude, unladylike girls," said Amy.

"And *I* hate affected, niminy-piminy little chits!" Jo responded, her hands shifting from behind her back and clenching into knotted fists.

"Birds in their little nests should all agree," said Hannah, their faithful servant, from the kitchen. Although Hannah had been with the family since even Meg could remember, her austere presence impelled both sharp voices to soften to gentle laughs.

"Really, girls, you are both to be blamed," said Meg, lecturing in her elder-sisterly fashion. "You are old enough to leave off boyish tricks and playing with your pet rat. You should have learned by now how to behave better, Josephine."

"I *don't* like being called *Josephine!*"

"That's why I call you that," Meg replied. "Such manners didn't matter so much when you were a little girl, but now you are grown. You should remember that you are a young lady."

"I am *not!* I'll wear my hair in pigtails until I'm twenty," cried Jo, pulling off her hair net and shaking down a lengthy chestnut mane. "I hate to think I've got to grow up and be 'Miss March,' and wear gowns and always look prim and proper. If I must be a girl, I wish I had never been born."

"Hush … to say such things," whispered Beth from the darkness, her eyes wide and empty.

Frustrated, Jo picked up her yarn and needles, and shook the blue army sock till the needles rattled like castanets. Then she flung the lot of them to the other side of the room, her ball of yarn bouncing as it unspooled across the floor.

"Poor Jo," sighed Beth, shifting forward. Her body was translucent against the firelight as she reached out and tried to stroke Jo's head with a hand that even death could not make ungentle. "It's too bad, but it can't be helped. So you must try to be content with making your name sound boyish and playing brother to your sisters."

"As for you, Amy," continued Meg, "you are altogether too particular and prim. Such airs are funny when you're young, but you'll grow up soon enough to be an affected little goose if you're not careful. And your absurd use of words is as bad as Jo's boyish slang."

"If Jo is a tomboy and Amy a goose, then what am I?" asked Beth, ready to share the discussion. But not one of the sisters heard her or, if they did, not one of them bothered or had the heart to respond. After a lengthy silence, Beth whispered ever so softly, "Can anybody hear me?"

The clock struck six, and after helping Hannah sweep the hearth, Amy placed a pair of slippers on the fender to warm up for Marmee. Somehow the sight of the old shoes had a good effect upon the girls, for they knew that Marmee would be home soon, and everyone brightened to welcome her. Meg stopped lecturing and lighted the lamps while Amy got out of the easy chair without being asked.

After recovering and rewinding her ball of blue yarn, Jo forgot how tired she was and held the slippers nearer to the blaze to warm them all the quicker.

"These slippers are quite worn out," said Jo wistfully. "Marmee must have new ones for Christmas."

"I thought I'd get her a pair with my dollar," said Amy.

"I'm the oldest," began Meg, but Jo cut her off with a decided, "Well, *I'm* the man of the family while Father is away, and perhaps I shall buy the slippers. Father told me to take special care of Mother while he was gone."

"I'll tell you what we'll do," said Meg. "Let's each of us get her something for Christmas, and not get anything for ourselves."

"That's so like you, dear!" exclaimed Jo. "What shall we get?"

Everyone thought soberly for a minute until Jo announced, as if the idea was suggested by the sight of her own glove-covered hands, "I shall buy her a nice new pair of kid gloves."

"How nice," said Meg, "when you are in such need to replace your own, which are so dreadfully stained."

Jo immediately hid her gloved hands behind her back.

"She wants nothing more than to see Father," whispered Beth from the darkness, although by their reactions, one would guess that none of her sisters heard her.

"Glad to find you so merry, my darling girls," said a cheery voice at the door, and the girls all turned to welcome their Marmee. Hannah watched this exchange from the kitchen, silent and as inscrutable as always. Marmee was not elegantly dressed, but she was a noble-looking woman nonetheless, and the girls thought the gray cloak and unfashionable bonnet covered the most splendid mother in the whole world.

"Well, my dears," Marmee said. "How have you got along today? There was so much to do, getting the boxes ready to ship out tomorrow, that I didn't come home to dinner. Has anyone come by? How is your cold, Meg? And you, Jo— you look tired to death. Come and kiss me, kiss me, my babies."

While making these maternal inquiries, Mrs. March got her wet things off, her warm slippers on, and sat down in the easy chair. Amy climbed into her lap, preparing to enjoy the happiest hour of her busy day while the other girls flew about, trying to make things comfortable for Marmee, each in her own way. Meg arranged the tea table, and Jo fetched more firewood from outside. Amy gave directions, as though her two sisters were her hired servants. And Beth reached out longingly to caress her loving mother's face, but her hands passed like smoke through Marmee.

As they gathered about the table and Hannah served them, Mrs. March said, with a particularly happy face, "I've got a treat for all of you."

A quick, bright smile went round like a streak of sunshine. Jo tossed up her napkin and cried, "A letter from Father! Three cheers!"

"Yes," said Marmee, "it's a nice long letter."

"How is he faring?" asked Meg, her brow creased with dark worry.

Marmee smiled and said, "He fares well, children, and thinks he shall get through the cold season better than we feared. He sends his loving wishes for Christmas, and an especial message to you girls."

"I think it is so splendid of Father to serve as chaplain even though he was too old to be drafted, and not strong enough to be a soldier," said Meg warmly.

"Don't I wish I could go as a soldier," exclaimed Jo. "Or perhaps a nurse, if I must, just so I could be near Father and help him."

"It must be very disagreeable, to sleep in a tent and eat all sorts of foul-tasting things and drink out of a tin mug," sighed Amy.

"When will he come home, Marmee?" asked Beth, with a little quiver in her voice.

Mrs. March paused, her expression falling. The room fairly pulsed with expectation until she said, quite seriously, "Father has been ill." Small gasps of shock and concern filled the room. "Once he recovered, he wanted to stay and continue his work as long as the war lasts, but he has been discharged and is on his way home."

Squeals of delight now filled the parlor. Meg clapped her hands daintily while Jo clenched her gloved fist and thundered forth several hearty "*Huzzahs!*" while Amy fanned her face as though she were about to faint.

From her corner by the fireplace, Beth whispered something, but nobody heard her voice, drowned as it was in the cacophony of excitement at the news.

"Oh, joy!" Meg cried. "Shall we really see him soon?"

"I expect him before Christmas morning," Marmee replied as she eased herself back into her chair and, closing her eyes, soon fell asleep in the warmth of the fire and her loving family.

"Jo! Jo! Where are you?" cried Meg at the foot of the garret stairs.

"Up here!" Jo answered from above. This was followed by the sound of running feet on the narrow stairs. Jo was wrapped in a comforter on an old sofa by the window, eating an apple and reading a novel, *The Heir of Radclyffe*. Outside, the sky was overcast and threatening more snow before Christmas, which was now three days away.

The garret was Jo's favorite refuge, especially on glowering days. She loved to retire here with an apron full of apples or a piece of cheese, when the family could afford it, and a nice book, to enjoy the quiet and the society of her pet rat, Scrabble, who lived inside the attic walls. Only for Scrabble would Jo remove the linen gloves from her hands and allow him to nip her flesh with tiny, stinging bites and then lap up the trickles of blood that flowed.

When Meg appeared, breathless, in the doorway, Jo lowered her book, irritated by the interruption. Scrabble whisked back into his rat hole, his small, beady eyes glaring at Meg from the safety of the den.

Jo waited to hear the news.

"Such fun! Only see! A regular note of invitation from Mrs. Gardiner for tomorrow night!" cried Meg, waving a thin piece of parchment, and then proceeding to read from it with girlish delight. "'Mrs. Gardiner would be happy to see Miss March and Miss Josephine at a little *soirée* tomorrow evening.' A *soirée*, Jo! Just imagine! Marmee has already agreed we can go. Now, what shall we wear?"

"What's the use of asking when you know we shall wear our poplins because we haven't got anything else?" answered Jo with her mouth full of apple. A fresh spot of blood ran from the back of her left hand to her wrist.

"If I only had a silk dress," sighed Meg.

"I'm sure our poplins look like silk, and they are nice enough. Yours is as good as new, but—Oh, dear! I just remembered the burn and the tear in mine. Whatever shall I do? The burn shows badly, and I can't let any more fabric out."

"Then you must sit still all evening and keep your back to the wall. The front is all right. I shall have a new ribbon for my hair, and I'm sure Marmee will lend me her little pearl pin. My new slippers are lovely, and my gloves will have to do."

"Mine are spoiled with—" but here Jo stopped and put her hands behind her back so Meg would not see the fresh wounds. "I can't afford to buy any new ones, but I dare not go without."

"You can't ask Mother for new gloves," Meg said, frowning. "They are so expensive, and you are so careless. You have spoiled your new ones already, and she said she shouldn't get you any more this winter. Can you make do with what you have?"

"I can hold my hands behind my back so no one will know how stained my gloves are," Jo said. "That's the best I can do." She glanced at the fine white lines of scars and fresh scabs on her hands. The fresh cut tingled and was still oozing blood.

"Then I'll go without. I don't care what people say or think!" cried Jo, taking up her book again. "Now go and answer the note, and let me finish this splendid story."

So Meg went away to "accept with thanks," look over her dress, and sing blithely as she did up her one real lace frill while Jo finished her novel, her apple, and allowed Scrabble one final sip of fresh blood.

"Now is my sash right, Jo? And does my hair look nice?" asked Meg, as she turned from the mirror in Mrs. Gardiner's dressing room after a prolonged prink.

"I know I shall forget to behave myself," Jo replied. "If you see me doing anything wrong, just remind me by a wink, will you?" returned Jo, giving her collar a twitch and her head a hasty brush.

"Winking isn't ladylike. I'll lift my eyebrows if anything is wrong, and nod if you are all right. Now hold your shoulders straight, and take short steps, and don't shake hands if you are introduced to anyone." She needn't add that anyone Jo might shake hands with would notice the spots of blood on her gloves but was too polite to mention them.

"How do you learn all the proper ways? I never can."

Downstairs they went, feeling a trifle timid, for they seldom went to parties, and informal as this little gathering was, it was an event to them. Mrs. Gardiner, a stately old lady, greeted them kindly and handed them over to Sallie, the eldest of six daughters. Meg knew Sallie and was at her ease very soon, but Jo, who didn't care much for girls or silly gossip, stood about with her hands behind her back and her back carefully against the wall. She felt about as much out of place as a colt in a flower garden. Half a dozen lads were talking about skates in another part of the room, and she longed to join them, for skating was one of the joys of her life. She telegraphed her wish to Meg, but her sister's eyebrows shot up so alarmingly that she dared not stir. No one came to talk to her, and one by one, the group dwindled away until she was left quite alone.

She could not roam about and amuse herself, for the burned breadth of cloth and the stains on her gloves would show, so she stared at people rather forlornly until the dancing began. Meg was asked to dance at once, and she tripped about so briskly that none would have guessed the pain her shoes were causing her. A big red-headed youth approached Jo's corner and, fearing he meant to engage her in conversation, she slipped into a curtained recess, intending to peep out like Scrabble and enjoy herself in peace.

Unfortunately, another bashful person had chosen that same refuge. As the curtain fell behind her, she found herself face to face with the "Laurence boy."

"I didn't know anyone else was here," stammered Jo, preparing to back out as speedily as she had bounced in.

"Don't mind me," the boy said pleasantly enough, though he looked as startled as a rabbit. In the dim light of the alcove, his eyes held a curious golden glow, as if filled with flecks of metal, and his skin was unusually pale, even for mid-winter. "Stay if you like."

"Shan't I disturb you?"

"Not a bit." His teeth were wide and flat, and they glistened wetly when he smiled. Jo sensed an uncanniness about him that was both off-putting and attractive. "I don't know many people here and felt rather strange at first."

"So did I," replied Jo. "Don't go away, please, unless you'd rather."

The boy sat down again and looked at his shoes until Jo said, trying to be polite and easy, "I believe I've had the pleasure of seeing you before. You live next door to us, don't you?"

"I do," he replied as he looked at her and laughed outright, for Jo's prim manner struck him as rather funny.

That put Jo at her ease, and she laughed, too, as she said, in her heartiest way, "You arrived in town not long ago."

"Three weeks, to be exact," said the boy. "But I have already learned some things. For instance, I know you have a pet rat. Tell me, Miss March—how is he?" The boy's pale eyes shone with a peculiar intensity as if he were attempting to probe her thoughts.

"My—How do you know about my rat?" she asked, quickly shifting her blood-stained gloved hands behind her back.

The Laurence boy deigned not to reply to that, but after the awkward silence that followed, Jo continued, "He's getting along quite nicely, thank you, Mr. Laurence. But I am not Miss March. I'm only Jo."

"And I am not Mr. Laurence. I'm only Laurie."

"Laurie … Laurie Laurence. Such an odd name."

His eyes took on an amber tone which was impossible for Jo to read. Had she inadvertently insulted him?

"My first name is Theodore, but I don't like it, so I ask everyone to call me Laurie instead."

"I hate my name, too. It's so sentimental. I wish every one would say Jo instead of Josephine."

"I suspect if they don't, you could soundly thrash them," he said, a faint smile tugging at the corners of his mouth. Jo was suddenly sure that, although Laurie's shoulders were thin and slightly stooped, he had a look about him that communicated he could handily take care of himself.

"I can't thrash Aunt March, so I suppose I shall have to bear it when she calls me Josephine," said Jo with a resigned sigh.

"Do you like to dance, Jo?" asked Laurie, looking as if he thought the name suited her quite aptly.

"I like it well enough if there is plenty of room, and everyone is lively. In a place this small, I'm sure to upset something or tread on people's feet or do something positively dreadful, so I keep to myself and let Meg sail about. Do you dance?"

"Never. I recently arrived here and haven't been in people's company enough yet to know how you do things."

"Where have you been, then?" inquired Jo.

After some hesitation, Laurie said, "Abroad," but this seemed to be laden with more meaning than he was letting on.

"Abroad!" cried Jo. "Oh, do tell me about it! I love to hear people describe their travels abroad."

Laurie looked askance, his golden eyes glittering, and didn't seem to know where to begin, so Jo decided not to press the matter. She quite glowed with pleasure in this boy's presence. She decided on the spot that she liked the "Laurence boy," and she took several good looks at him so that she might describe him to the girls, for they had no brothers, very few male cousins, and boys were almost unknown creatures to them. Laurie, in particular, struck her as unique within the gender.

He had curly black hair, and pale, almost translucent skin. His large, oval-shaped eyes glittered like gold in the candlelight. His nose was handsome if narrow, and he had fine, wide teeth, though the canines appeared pointed and protruded more than usual. His hands and feet were small and slender, and he was taller than Jo and quite thin. Jo wondered how old he was, and it was on the tip of her tongue to ask, but she checked herself in time and, with unusual tact, tried to find out in a roundabout way.

"I suppose you are already pegging at college, then … I mean, studying hard." Jo blushed at her dreadful use of the word *pegging*, which had escaped her unawares.

Laurie smiled but didn't seem at all shocked. He answered with a shrug. "Not for a year or two yet. I won't go before I'm seventeen, in any event."

"Are you but fifteen, then?" asked Jo, looking at the tall lad.

"Sixteen of your years next month."

His curious use of the phrase *your years* slipped right past Jo, who commented, "How I wish I was going to college! But you don't look as if you like the prospect."

"I hate it. School is nothing but grinding or skylarking. I don't like the way fellows do either, on your pl— … in your country."

"What do you like to do, then?"

"Live and enjoy myself in my own way," replied Laurie mysteriously, "but I hope to return home soon."

Jo wanted very much to ask where "home" and what "his own way" were, but his lowering brows looked rather more threatening as he knit them together. She wanted to ask all about where he had been born and lived before coming to the States, but she changed the subject by saying, "That's a splendid polka. Why don't you go and try it?"

"Only if you will come, too," he answered with a gallant little bow.

"I can't, for I told Meg I wouldn't because …"

There Jo stopped herself and felt rather undecided whether to tell him the truth or merely to laugh it off.

"Because what?"

"Promise you won't tell?"

"I promise."

"Well, I scorched my dress quite badly, and though it's nicely mended, it still shows. Meg told me to keep still so no one would notice. You may go ahead and laugh, if you'd like. It *is* funny, I know."

But Laurie didn't laugh. He only looked down a minute, the expression on his face so puzzling that Jo began to wonder if he was having some kind of spell until he said very gently, "Never mind that, then." Then he brightened and added, "I'll tell you how we can manage. There's a long hall, and we can dance there, and no one will be the wiser."

He held his hand out to her, but she hesitated to bring her gloved hands around from behind her back. He couldn't help but see the blood stains on them.

Jo silently thanked him as he took her hand without batting an eye, and she gladly went with him, wishing she had two neat gloves like the nice pearl-colored ones he wore.

The hall was indeed empty, and they had a grand polka, for Jo danced well and quickly taught Laurie the steps, which he executed with some clumsiness she had the grace not to mention. When the music stopped, they sat down on the stairs so Jo could catch her breath. Laurie seemed unaffected by the physical activity and was just about to say something when Meg appeared. She beckoned to Jo, who reluctantly followed her sister into a side room, where she collapsed onto a sofa, holding onto her foot and looking pale and in pain.

"I've sprained my ankle dreadfully. That stupid high heel gave me a sad wrench. It aches so I can hardly stand, and I don't know how I'm ever going to get home." She rocked to and fro, wincing in pain.

"I knew you'd hurt your feet with those silly shoes," answered Jo, softly rubbing the poor ankle as she spoke. "I'm sorry, but I don't see what you can do except get a carriage or stay here for the night."

"I can't have a carriage without it costing us ever so much. I dare say I can't get one at all, for most people come in their own carriages, and it's a long way to the stable, and no one to send."

"I'll go."

"No, indeed! It's past nine, and dark as Egypt outside. I certainly can't stay here, for the house is full this evening. Sallie has some girls staying the night. I'll rest until Hannah comes, and then hobble home the best I can."

"I'll ask Laurie. He will go," said Jo, looking relieved as the idea occurred to her.

"Mercy, no! Don't ask him or anyone else. Get me my overshoes, and put these slippers with our things. I can't dance anymore, but as soon as supper is over, watch for Hannah and tell me the minute she arrives."

"They are going out to supper now. I'll stay with you. I'd rather."

"No, dear. Run along, and bring me some coffee. I'm so tired I can't stir."

So Meg reclined, and Jo went blundering away to the dining room, which she found after going into a china closet and opening the door of a room where old Mr. Gardiner was taking a little private refreshment. Making a dart at the table, she secured a cup of coffee, which she immediately spilled on her gloves.

"Oh, dear, what a blunderbuss I am!" exclaimed Jo.

"May I help?" inquired a friendly voice. And there was Laurie, with a full cup of coffee in one hand and a plate of ice in the other.

"I was getting something for Meg, who is terribly tired, and someone shook me, and here I am in a sorry state," answered Jo, glancing dismally at the coffee-colored glove. The warm fluid was scalding her hand, and she had no choice but to remove the glove, thus exposing her scarred hand and wrist.

"Oh, you poor dear," Laurie cried, taking her hand in his and touching it with a soothing caress that sent electricity through her. "You've gone and hurt yourself. Here. Come with me."

Before Jo could say a word, he whisked her along the hallway away from the crowd. When they stopped, he reached into his jacket pocket and removed a small black box. Upon closer inspection, Jo noted several small indentations on the side and a tiny green light, which Laurie directed at her hand. After he pressed a small button on the side of the box, a faint humming sound filled the air, and a cooling sensation embraced her hand and wrist like an unseen glove.

"Whatever are you doing?" Jo asked as the cool, prickling sensation ran up her hand and forearm. Ignoring her inquiry, Laurie attended to his business for a whispered count of ten, and then said simply, "That should suffice."

He replaced the small device into his jacket pocket and smiled at her.

"Your hand should feel better soon," he said, walking with her back to the dining table. "What do you say we bring a cup of coffee to your sister?"

"Oh—yes. Thank you. I would offer to take it myself, but I am sure I would get into another scrape."

Jo led the way, and as if used to waiting on ladies, Laurie drew up a little table, brought a second installment of coffee for Jo, and was so obliging that even critical

Meg pronounced him a "nice boy." Jo asked if he could use that curious device to aid her sister's twisted ankle, but he looked at her, silently scolding her as he shook his head, no.

While Meg rested her foot, they had a merry time and were in the midst of a game of *Buzz* with two or three other young people, who had strayed in, when Hannah appeared in the doorway. Meg forgot her foot and rose so quickly that she was forced to catch hold of Jo, with a brief exclamation of pain.

"Hush! Don't say anything about it," she whispered to Jo, adding aloud, "It's nothing. I turned my foot a little, that's all," and limped upstairs to put her things on.

Hannah's expression remained perfectly neutral when her eyes met Laurie's. Jo was sure something unspoken passed between their maid and her new friend, but for the life of her she couldn't tell what. Meg returned, limping, and Jo was at her wit's end until she decided to take things into her own hands. She ran out and found a servant and asked if he could provide them with a carriage. It happened to be a hired waiter who knew nothing about the neighborhood, and Jo was looking around for help when Laurie, who apparently had heard her request, came up and offered his grandfather's carriage, which had just come for him.

"It's so early. You can't mean to go yet?" began Jo.

"I always leave early. I do, truly. I find that I tire easily at such events."

Jo remembered the vigor with which he had danced and doubted the veracity of his claim, but she was pleased to let him take her sister and her home. "It's on my way," he added, "and, you know, it is supposed to snow, they say."

That settled it, and Jo gratefully accepted. Hannah hated the snow as much as a cat does, so she agreed although Jo caught another unspoken glance pass between Hannah and Laurie, which filled her with curiosity.

Once settled in the carriage, they rolled away feeling very festive and elegant. Laurie rode on the box with the driver so Meg could keep her foot up on the seat next to Hannah.

"I had a capital time. Did you?" asked Jo, rumpling up her hair and making herself comfortable.

"I did," said Meg, "until I hurt myself. Sallie's friend, Annie Moffat, took a fancy to me and asked me to spend a week with her family in Boston. She is going in the spring when the opera comes to the city. It will be perfectly splendid if Marmee will let me go."

"I saw you dancing with the red-headed man I ran away from," said Jo. "Was he nice?"

"Oh, quite. But his hair is auburn, not red, and he was very polite."

"He looked like a grasshopper having a fit. Laurie and I couldn't help but laugh. Did you hear us?"

"No, but it was very rude to laugh. What were you about all that time, hiding away there? It's unladylike."

Jo told her adventures but failed to mention the small act of healing Laurie had accomplished on her injured hand. She thrilled at the memory of his touch when he held her hand to inspect the burn. Before they knew it, they were home. With many thanks, they said good night to Laurie and crept in, hoping to disturb no one.

"What in the world are you going to do now, Jo?" asked Meg as her sister came tramping through the hall wearing heavy rubber boots, an old sack, and a hood. She had a broom in one hand and a shovel in the other.

"Going out for exercise," answered Jo with a mischievous twinkle in her eyes.

"I should think it's cold and dreary enough outside, and I advise you to stay warm and dry by the fire, as I do," said Meg with a shiver.

"Never take advice! Can't keep still all day, and not being a pussycat, I don't like to doze by the fire. I like adventures, and I'm going to find one."

With Beth watching from the shadows, Meg went back to toasting her feet and reading *Ivanhoe* while Jo went outside to dig a path in the snow with great energy. Her shovel soon cleared a path all round the garden for Amy to walk in when the sun came out. Father would be pleased to see such industry. Now, the garden separated the Marches' house from that of Mr. Laurence. Both stood in a suburb of Concord, which was still country-like, with groves and lawns, large gardens, and quiet streets. A low hedge parted the two properties. On one side was an old, brown house, looking rather bare and shabby, robbed of the grape vines that in summer covered its walls and the flowers, which surrounded it. On the other side was a stately stone mansion, plainly betokening every sort of creature comfort, from the big coach house and well-kept grounds to the conservatory and the glimpses of lovely things one caught between the rich curtains.

Yet it seemed a lonely, lifeless sort of house, thought Jo, for no children frolicked on the lawn, no motherly face smiled at the window, and few people went in and out except for the old gentleman and his grandson, Laurie.

To Jo's lively fancy, this fine house seemed an enchanted palace full of remarkable splendors and delights, which no one enjoyed. She had long wanted to behold these hidden glories and to know the Laurence boy. Talking with him at the party had only enhanced his attraction. He had only recently arrived to reside with his grandfather. The story, as Jo had heard it, was that he had studied in Europe following the death of his parents, although he had not mentioned such an event last night.

Since the party, Jo had been more eager than ever to know him, and she had planned ways of making friends with him, but she had not seen him outside today, and she began to think he may have gone away. Earlier in the day, though, she had spied a pale face in an upper window, looking wistfully down into their yard.

"That boy is suffering from a lack of society and fun," she said to herself. "He keeps himself shut up all day as if he's afraid of the sun. He needs somebody young and lively to associate with. I've a mind to go over and tell him so!"

The idea amused Jo, who liked to do daring things and was always scandalizing Meg by her peculiar performances. The plan of "going over there" was not forgotten. And when the snowy afternoon came, Jo resolved to try what could be done. She waited to see Mr. Laurence drive off, and then she sallied forth to dig her way down to the hedge, where she paused and took a survey.

All was quiet. The curtains were down at the lower windows, and the servants were out of sight. Nothing human was visible but a curly black head leaning on a thin hand in an upper window.

"Poor boy," thought Jo. "All alone on this dismal day. It's a shame. I'll toss up a snowball and make him look at me, and then say a kind word."

Up went a handful of soft snow, and the head turned at once, showing a face which lost its listless expression in an instant as the big eyes brightened and the wide mouth smiled. Jo waved, laughing as she flourished her shovel and called out—

"How do you do? Are you sick?"

Up went the window sash, and Laurie croaked out as hoarsely as a raven, "Better, thank you. I've had a bad cold since the night of the party and have been shut up."

"I'm sorry to hear that. What do you for amusement?"

"Nothing. It's as dull as tombs up here."

"Don't you read?"

"Not much. Grandfather won't let me."

"Can't somebody read to you?"

"No one will."

"Have someone come and see you, then."

"There isn't anyone I'd like to see. Boys make such a row, and my head is weak."

"Isn't there some nice girl who'd read to you? Girls are quiet and like to play nurse."

"I don't know any."

"You know me," said Jo. She started to laugh but then stopped.

"So I do," cried Laurie. "Will you come up, please?"

"I'm not quiet *or* nice, but I'll come up if Mother will allow. I'll ask. Shut the window, like a good boy. You'll catch your death. Wait until I come."

With that, Jo shouldered her shovel like a musket and marched into the house. Laurie was in a rush of excitement at the idea of having company, and he flew about to get ready, tidying up his room, which in spite of half a dozen servants was anything but neat.

Presently there came a loud ring at the door and then a decided voice, asking for "Master Laurie." A surprised-looking servant came running up to announce a young lady.

"Show her up, please. It's Miss Jo," said Laurie, going to the door of his little parlor to meet Jo, who appeared looking rosy and quite at ease with a covered dish in her gloved hands.

"Here I am, bag and baggage," she said briskly. "Mother sends her love and was glad if I could do anything for you. Meg wanted me to bring some of her blanc-mange. She makes it very nicely."

"That looks too pretty to eat," he said, smiling with pleasure as Jo uncovered the dish and showed the blancmange, surrounded by a garland of green leaves and the scarlet flowers of Amy's pet geranium.

"Tell the girl to put it away for your tea," said Jo. "It's so simple you can eat it and, being soft, it will slip down without hurting your sore throat. What a cozy room this is."

"It might be if it was kept nice, but the maids are so lazy, and I dare say I don't know how to make them mind."

"I'll straighten it up in two minutes, for it only needs to have the hearth brushed, and the things made straight on the mantelpiece, and the books put here, and the bottles there, and your sofa turned from the light, and the pillows plumped. Now then, you're fixed."

And so he was, for, as she talked, Jo had whisked about the room putting things into place which, when done, gave quite a different air to the room. She noticed a few objects and artifacts that struck her as unique, but she had the manners not to remark on them. One, a photograph of a lovely woman with long, black hair, seemed to be three-dimensional, to which Jo ascribed a trick of the eye. Laurie watched her in respectful silence, and when she beckoned him to his sofa, he sat down with a sigh of satisfaction.

"How kind you are," he said graciously. "Yes, that's exactly what it needed. Now, please take the big chair, and let me do something to amuse you."

"I came to amuse you," Jo said, habitually placing her gloved hands behind her back to hide the stains. "Shall I read aloud?" She looked affectionately toward some inviting books in a case nearby. Several titles, written on the spines, appeared to be in a language unfamiliar to her, perhaps Arabic or Hindoo, she thought.

"Thank you, but I've read all those, and if you don't mind, I'd rather talk," answered Laurie.

"Not a bit. I'll talk all day if you'll only set me going. Beth used to say I never know when to stop."

"The pretty one is Meg, and the curly-haired one is Amy, but I don't believe I have met or seen your sister Beth."

"Beth is—" began Jo, but she fell silent, not sure how to proceed until she ended with a feeble, "We speak very little of her."

Laurie colored up but said frankly, "Why, you see, I often hear you calling to one another, and when I'm alone upstairs, I can't help but look over at your house. You always seem to be having such grand times. I beg your pardon for being so rude, but sometimes you forget to pull the curtain at the window where the flowers are, and when the lamps are lighted, it's like looking at a living picture book to see you all gathered around with your mother. Her face looks so sweet behind the flowers. I can't help watching. I haven't got any mother, you know."

"I'm so sorry," replied Jo. "I didn't know. Do you care to tell me what happened?"

"She was from … Italy. When she died, my father, being unable to raise me on his own because his business concerns take him far and wide, sent me to Concord to live with my grandfather until I begin college."

Laurie poked at the fire to hide a slight twitching of the upper lip and a certain moistness in his eyes that he could not control.

The solitary, yearning look in his eyes went straight to Jo's heart. She had been so simply taught that there was no nonsense in her head, and at fifteen she was as innocent and frank as any child. Laurie was ill and lonely, and she was grateful for how rich she truly was in home and true happiness. She gladly wished to share it with him. Her face was very friendly, and her sharp voice unusually gentle as she said—

"We'll never draw that curtain any more, and I give you leave to look as much as you like. I just wish, though, instead of peeping, you'd come over and visit. Mother is so splendid. She'd do you heaps of good, and we'd welcome you and have jolly times. Wouldn't your grandpa let you?"

"I think he would if your mother asked," replied Laurie. "He's very kind, though he does not look so. He lets me do whatever I like, pretty much, only he's afraid I might be a bother to strangers."

"We are not strangers. We are neighbors. And you needn't worry you'd be a bother to us. We want to know you. I've been wanting to meet you ever so long. We have got acquainted with all our neighbors save you."

"Well, you see, Grandpa lives among his books and doesn't mind much what happens outside. Mr. Brooke, my tutor, doesn't live here, so I have no one to go about with me, so I just stay at home and get on as best I can until I can return."

"Return?"

"Return home," said Laurie and, like on the night of the party, Jo had the good manners not to pursue the discussion if he seemed unwilling. But even as he said this, Jo could sense the well of sadness inside him, and the thought that he felt he didn't belong anywhere or to anyone cut her deeply.

"You ought to make an effort to go visit everywhere you are asked. Then, perhaps, you'll have plenty of friends and pleasant places to go. Never mind being bashful. It won't last long."

Laurie wasn't offended by Jo's forthright manner, for there was so much goodwill in her that it was impossible not to take her blunt speeches as kindly as they were meant.

"Do you like your school?" asked the boy, changing the subject after a brief pause during which he stared at the fire, and Jo looked all around her.

"I don't go to school," she answered. "I'm a business-man ... business-girl, I mean. I wait on my Aunt March, and a dear, cross old soul she is, too."

Laurie opened his mouth to ask a question, but remembering just in time that it wasn't polite manners to make too many inquiries into others' affairs, shut it again, content that Jo didn't probe too deeply into his family story, either. He found her freshness and openness charming and irresistible and might lower his guard and say more than he should if he wasn't careful.

For her part, Jo liked his obvious good breeding, and she didn't mind having a laugh at Aunt March, so she gave him a lively description of the fidgety old lady, her fat poodle, the parrot that spoke Spanish, and the library where she reveled when Aunt March was napping. They got to talking about books, and to Jo's delight, she found that Laurie loved books as well as she did and had read even more than herself.

"If you like books so much, please come downstairs and see ours. Grandfather is out on business, so you needn't be afraid," said Laurie, getting up. He looked unsteady on his feet, and when he took a breath, Jo noticed a most unusual whistling sound, but she chose not to comment on it.

"I'm not afraid of anything," Jo said with a toss of the head.

"I don't believe you are," exclaimed the boy, looking at her with much admiration, though he privately thought she would have good reason to be a trifle afraid of the old gentleman if she met him when in one of his moods.

Laurie led the way from room to room, letting Jo stop to examine whatever struck her fancy. And so, at last they came to the library, where she clapped her gloved hands as she always did when especially delighted. The walls were lined with books, and there were pictures and statues, and distracting little cabinets full of strange coins and other curiosities. There were Sleepy Hollow chairs, and queer tables, and bronzes, and—best of all—a great open fireplace with Italian tiles lined all round it.

"What richness," sighed Jo, sinking into the depth of a purple velour chair and gazing about her with an air of intense satisfaction. "Theodore Laurence, you ought to be the happiest boy in the world."

"A fellow can't live on books alone," said Laurie, shaking his head as he perched on a table opposite and regarded her with his curious golden eyes. In the dimness of the room, they held a vibrant glow to which Jo found herself drawn.

Before he could say more, a bell rang, and Jo flew up, exclaiming with alarm, "Mercy me! It's your grandpa!"

"What if it is?" Laurie said. "I thought you were not afraid of anything."

"I think I am afraid of him a little bit, but I don't know why I should be. Marmee said I might come, and I don't think you're any the worse for it," Jo said, composing herself as she kept her eyes on the door.

"I'm a great deal the better for it, and ever so much obliged. I'm only afraid you are very tired of talking to me," said Laurie gratefully.

A maid appeared in the doorway and said, "The doctor to see you, sir."

"Would you mind if I left you for a minute?" said Laurie.

"Don't mind me. I'm happy as a cricket here," answered Jo, although truth to tell, she was curious to ask Laurie why he didn't use on himself the same strange healing device he had used on her parboiled hand at the party. But she let the thought slip away and watched as Laurie left the room.

While he was gone, Jo amused herself in her own way. She was standing before a fine portrait of the old gentleman when the door opened again and, without turning, she said decidedly, "I'm sure now that I should be afraid of him, for he's got cruel, dark eyes, and his mouth is altogether grim. He looks as if he has a tremendous will of his own."

"Thank you, ma'am, for that analysis," said a growling voice behind her, and there, to her great dismay, stood old Mr. Laurence. Unlike his grandson, he was squarely built, with short legs and thick, powerful arms. His eyes were as dark as ink wells.

Poor Jo blushed until she couldn't blush any redder, and her heart beat uncomfortably fast in her thin chest as she thought what she had done. Feeling terribly alone and vulnerable, she felt a wild desire to run away, but that was cowardly, so she resolved to stand her ground and get out of this as best she could. A second look showed her that the living eyes, under the bushy eyebrows, were kinder than the painted ones, and was there a sly twinkle in them. The gruff voice was gruffer than ever, as the old gentleman said after the dreadful pause, "So, you say that you're afraid of me, hey?"

"No—no, sir," Jo replied, knowing in her heart that he knew she was not telling the truth.

"And you don't think me as handsome as your grandfather?"

"Not quite, begging your pardon, sir."

"And I've got a tremendous will, have I?"

"I only said I suspect so," Jo stammered.

That final answer seemed to please the old gentleman, for he threw his head back and gave a short, barking laugh and reached out to shake hands with her. His palm, she noticed, was as rough as tree bark, which struck her as odd, seeing as it was the hand of a gentleman.

Putting his finger under her chin, he turned her face up and examined it gravely for a long time. Looking directly at him, and so close, she could see now the same golden glint in his eyes as in Laurie's. After a lengthening moment of intense scrutiny, he let her face go, saying with a nod, "You've got your grandfather's spirit, I dare say, even if you haven't got his face."

"Thank you, sir," said Jo.

"What have you been doing to this boy of mine, hey?" was the next question, sharply put.

"Only trying to be neighborly, sir."

"Neighborly, you say?"

"I wanted to cheer him up in his illness."

"His illness is no concern of yours," the old gentleman replied. "So you think he needs cheering?"

"Yes, sir. A bit, sir. He seems a bit lonely, and being around young folks would do him no end of good. We are only girls, my sisters and I, but we should be glad to help if we could," said Jo eagerly.

"Tut, tut, tut! And what news of your father?"

"We received a letter just the other day, informing us that he will be home in time for Christmas."

"What a fine Christmas present that will be," replied Mr. Laurence. "I, myself, was born on Christmas Day."

Jo had no idea how to respond to that, having heard that people who have the audacity to be born on the Savior's birthday are fated to be evil. She noticed the sudden darkness in his eyes, as if a cloud had shifted in front of the sun, blocking its warming rays.

"Hey! Why? What the dickens has come to the fellow?" said the old gentleman as Laurie came running downstairs and was brought up with a start of surprise at the astounding sight of Jo standing in front of his redoubtable grandfather.

"I didn't know you'd come home, sir," Laurie began.

"That's evident by the way you racket downstairs. Come. Behave like a gentleman." He cast a wary eye at Jo, and then added, "Perhaps young master will make the adjustment to his life here after all."

Laurie's face colored at this, and she didn't need to hear him say how much he wanted to go back home, wherever home was.

Turning to Jo, the old gentleman continued, "You're right on the money, Miss March. The lad is lonely so dreadfully far away from home. Perhaps we'll see what these little girls next door can do for him."

Jo determined it was time to go, but Laurie said he had one more thing to show her, and he took her away to the conservatory, which had been lighted for her benefit. It seemed quite fairy-like to Jo as she went up and down the walks, enjoying the blooming walls on either side, the soft light, the sweet, damp air, and the wonderful vines and trees that grew in profusion. Some of them she didn't recognize at all, and many had strange fruits on their vines and thorns on their stems. They filled the air with an intoxicatingly unearthly perfume, which hung about her while her new friend cut the finest flowers until his hands were full. Then he tied them up, saying with a happy look, "Please give these to your cherished mother, and tell her I approve of the medicine she sent to me."

"That will do. That will do, young man," said the old gentleman who was standing in the doorway of the conservatory. Jo had not heard him enter. "Too many sugarplums are not good for her. Going, Miss March? Well, I hope you will come again. Give my respects to your mother."

He bowed deeply to her, but even with his head bowed, he looked at her, and she could tell that something of a sudden had not pleased him. When they got into the hall, Jo whispered to Laurie, asking if she had said or done anything amiss. He shook his head.

"No. It was I. He doesn't like it when I enter the conservatory."

"Why not?"

"I'll tell you another day."

"Take care of yourself, then."

"I will, but will you come again, I hope?"

"Only if you promise to come and visit us, if you are well enough. Perhaps on Christmas day."

"Perhaps I shall."

"Good night, Laurie."

"And a good night to you, too, Doctor Jo."

᙭   ᙭

When all the afternoon's adventures had been told, the family felt inclined to go visiting in a body, for each found something very attractive in the big house on the other side of the hedge. Mrs. March wanted to talk of her father with the old man who had known him. Meg longed to walk in the flower conservatory and see its exotic beauties, as described by Jo. Amy was eager to see the fine paintings and statues. And Beth sighed from the corner and whispered how she wished she could play the grand piano.

"Mother, what did he mean by that nice little speech he gave about the medicine Mother sent him?" asked Jo. "Did he mean the blancmange?"

"How silly you are, child," Marmee replied. "He meant you, of course."

"He did?"

And Jo opened her eyes as if it had never occurred to her.

"I never saw such a girl! You don't know a compliment when you receive one," said Meg with the air of a young lady who knew all about such matters.

"I think they are a great nonsense, and I'll thank you not to be silly and spoil my fun. Laurie's a nice boy, and I like him, and I won't have any sentimental stuff about compliments and such rubbish spoil my fun. We'll all be good to him because he hasn't got any parents, and he may come over and see us. Mayn't he, Marmee?"

"Yes, Jo. Your friend is very welcome here, and I hope Meg will remember that children should be children as long as they can."

"I don't call myself a child, and I'm not in my teens yet," observed Amy.

"And I say to be a child again would be a lovely thing … a heavenly thing," whispered Beth from her dark corner beside the fireplace. Only she noticed the way their servant Hannah was standing, unseen and silent, in the doorway, her eyes cast in deep concern.

As Christmas approached, the usual mysteries began to haunt the house, and Jo frequently convulsed the family by proposing utterly impossible or magnificently absurd ceremonies in honor of this unusually merry Christmas they faced this year with Father's promised return. She was impracticable and would have had bonfires, skyrockets, and triumphal arches, if she had her own way. After many skirmishes and snubbings, her extravagant plans were effectually quenched, and she went about with a forlorn face as she retired to the garret where she allowed Scrabble to feed on more blood than was his wont.

Snow arrived the day before Christmas and continued overnight, piling up three feet or more in the country roads and fields. Christmas Day morning dawned dark and gloomy, but the family was determined to spend their day in cozy companionship, except for Jo, who planned to spend some time with Laurie.

Perhaps because of the weather, perhaps because of her uncanny insight, Hannah felt "in her bones" that the day was going to be an unusually bad day, and she proved herself a true prophetess, for everybody and everything seemed bound to go wrong, no matter what one attempted. To begin with, Father had written more than a month ago from the Army hospital in Maryland that he expected to be home soon. Meg thought it would be exquisite if he were to arrive before they shared their holiday dinner, which Hannah took all day to prepare with help from all three girls. But with the weather choking the roads, Marmee expressed her doubts about his arrival before the New Year.

Beth felt uncommonly uneasy that morning, and with the cloudy sky casting such darkness, she shifted from her dark corner by the fireplace to the window, where she looked out with the most forlorn expression possible at the storm, which was now a raging blizzard.

On Christmas Day, the little women had outdone their best efforts to be festive, for, like elves, they had gotten up before dawn and conjured up a comical surprise. Out in the garden stood a stately snowman, crowned with Father's old top hat and bearing a sweet potato for a nose and two lumps of charred wood for eyes, and a castoff scarf wrapped around his neck. Even before the work was done, a layer of snow obscured the features, so carefully molded. After breakfast, when Marmee and Hannah looked out at it, it was nothing more or less than a shapeless hump of pure white mounted by an old beaver top hat.

Jo finally came out of her gloom when Laurie arrived in the evening after their Christmas meal, having trudged through the snow to be with them and bearing gifts. And what ridiculous speeches he made as he presented each gift to the family members.

"I'm so full of happiness," said Meg, once the presents were dispensed and the holiday treats of sugar cookies and dried fruit were consumed. As evening drew on, the storm intensified, whistling under the eaves, and each one of them had given up any hope that Father would arrive to share the blessed day in the warmth and comfort of his loving family.

"I would be truly happy if only Father were here," sighed Beth, who had returned to her corner upon the arrival of the strange boy from next door. She sensed he knew she was there, even though he never once looked directly at her. She watched with empty eyes as the festivities continued, such as they were, but by this time each and every one of the celebrants was exhausted.

"So would I," added Jo, slapping the pocket wherein reposed the long-desired edition of *The Marble Fawn* she had so wanted.

"I'm sure I am," echoed Amy, poring over the engraved copy of the Madonna and Child, which her mother had given her in a pretty frame.

"Of course I am," cried Meg, smoothing the silvery folds of her first silk dress, for Mr. Laurence had insisted on giving it to her.

"How can I be otherwise?" said Mrs. March gratefully, as her eyes went from her husband's letter to her children's smiling faces, and her hand caressed the brooch made of gray and golden, chestnut and dark brown hair, which the girls had fastened on her dress.

Now and then, however, in this workaday world, things do happen in the delightful storybook fashion, and what a comfort it is when they do. Half an hour after everyone had said they were so happy they could only hold one drop more, that drop came. Laurie had bid them all a goodnight and, wrapped in jacket and scarf, had left by the parlor door. But he was gone for no more than a minute when there came a heavy knocking on the door. Without being invited, he popped his head in very quietly. He might just as well have turned a somersault and uttered an Indian war whoop, for his face was so full of excitement and his voice so treacherously joyful that everyone jumped up, though he only said, in a queer, breathless voice, "Here's another Christmas present for the March family."

Before the words were well out of his mouth, he was whisked away somehow, and in his place stood a tall man, muffled to the eyes, who tried to say something but couldn't. His face was gaunt and gray beneath the scarf, and his eyes held a surprising glint of gold, even in the dimly lit room. Hannah, in the kitchen cleaning up after the festivities, uttered a loud gasp of surprise.

Of course, there was a general stampede, and for several minutes everybody seemed to lose their wits, for the strangest things were done, and no one said a word.

Mr. March became invisible in the embrace of three pairs of loving arms. Jo disgraced herself by nearly fainting and had to be doctored by Laurie in the hallway. Meg clasped her hands and let out a whoop of joy that was more befitting Jo, while Amy, the dignified, tumbled over a stool and, never stopping to get up, hugged and cried over her father's snow-covered boots in the most touching manner. Mrs. March was the first to recover herself. She held up her hand with a warning and said, "Hush, children! Remember Beth."

But it was too late.

The figure by the fireplace loomed closer, but then, upon making eye contact with the bundled figure, suddenly shrank back, an expression not of joy but of stark terror on her face. She uttered a low, lonely wail that mingled with the wind in the flue.

"That's not Father," she whispered, but in the ensuing chaos of Father's arrival, not one of them heard her, or, if they did, no one deigned to listen to, much less believe her.

It was not at all romantic, for Hannah was discovered standing in the kitchen doorway, her eyes wide and glistening, her face also a mask of fright that matched Beth's, which had dissolved into the darkness next to the fireplace.

"Why, what is it, dear Hannah?" asked Meg, who was the first to notice the shocked expression on their loving maid's face.

But Hannah found she could say nothing, her tongue was tied into a knot as she regarded Mr. March, all the while shaking her head from side to side and buzzing so loudly Jo was reminded of the sounds hornets might make in their hive. Her eyes narrowed with what could only have been doubt and a rising concern.

Marmee suddenly remembered that Mr. March needed rest and sustenance after what must have been a terribly grueling ordeal through the teeth of the storm, but she paused when she removed her husband's glove and took hold of his hands, squeezing them between her own.

"My Goodness, how cold you are," she said, feeling her own share of concern because she realized that her husband had not spoken a word of greeting. "Come," she said. "Sit by the fire and warm yourself."

Father looked at her with a vague, uncomprehending glance and said nothing as he walked with halting steps over to the nearest chair.

"Aren't you going to sit in your customary chair, Father?" asked Amy, indicating the old wooden rocker with the padded cushions that was placed front and center of the blazing fireplace.

Father stood in the middle of the room, looking mutely at her as though he had no understanding whatsoever of what she had just said. His gaze then wandered around the small parlor with the most mystified expression painted upon his gaunt and pale features. Mrs. March could only shudder at the thought of the ordeals he must have endured since last she had seen him. She noted now that his eyes remained clouded and uncomprehending, as though he were dazed.

All the while, Mr. March spoke not, but he forced a crooked smile when he looked at his wife, exposing wide, white teeth that, in the firelight, looked much larger than anyone remembered. After a glance at Meg, who was violently poking the fire, he looked at his wife again with an inquiring lift of the eyebrows. Mrs. March gently nodded and asked, rather abruptly, if he wouldn't like to have something to eat and drink. Jo saw and understood the look, and she stalked away to get a bottle of wine and some beef tea, muttering to herself as she closed the kitchen door behind her. There, she locked eyes with Hannah, whose expression of shock had abated not at all.

"Why, what ever is the matter, Hannah?" she asked.

Hannah did not respond. She stood immobile and shook her head from side to side and whispered softly, "Beth is right."

Meanwhile, back in the parlor, Amy, who now sat on her father's knee, whispered, "I'm glad it's over because now we've got you back."

"That's not Father," Beth repeated, unseen from the darkness in the corner. Her voice was as soft as the hush of falling snow outside.

"Rather a rough road for you to travel," Mrs. March said to her husband. "Especially the latter part of it in such weather. But you have got on bravely, and your burdens are in a fair way to tumble off very soon." She looked with motherly satisfaction at the young faces gathered around her husband and thought how the worst of their trials, too, must now be close to an end.

"Our troubles are just beginning," said Hannah, who entered from the kitchen a step ahead of Jo, who was carrying a bottle of wine and a steaming cup of beef tea.

"What do you mean?" inquired Marmee, casting a furtive glance at the maid who was moving forward, inching her way as if traversing a pit filled with snakes.

Hannah did not answer her as she cast a long, meaningful glance at Laurie, who throughout the reunion had graciously remained silent and watchful by the door.

"You see it, too, do you not, young Master Laurence?" Hannah asked, turning her full attention on the boy whose first impulse was to fade back into the darkness even if it meant going back out into the fury of the blizzard without his coat and scarf snuggly wrapped around him.

"Tell me. You see it. Don't you?" Hannah said as she took several strides toward him.

Mrs. March and the three girls watched in awe, their attention fixed on these two. Speaking up so forcefully was quite uncharacteristic of Hannah, but Laurie remained perfectly silent for a terribly long moment, his golden eyes flashing back and forth from Mrs. March to each of the girls, including Beth in the corner, and then finally at Father, sitting in his chair. Ever so slightly, he nodded and said, "He is not who I thought he was."

The expression on Hannah's face suddenly fixed with determination as she shifted her gaze again to Father and stared intently at him. Her unblinking eyes held a golden glint, like a cat's eyes in the firelight.

"He's not of our kind," Hannah said.

"Whatever are you two talking about?" inquired Meg, wringing her hands together helplessly, but Hannah said not another word. Instead, with stunning agility, she moved quickly, closing the distance between herself and the gaunt fig-ure shivering in the chair beside the fireplace.

In other circumstances, had he not been so exhausted from his travels, Meg thought, Father would have reacted in time. But his journey home had worn him past the point of exhaustion, and his only reaction was to let out a high-pitched squealing sound as the maid came up close to him and clasped him by the shoul-ders with both hands. Then, with a surprising display of strength, she lifted him to his feet, spun him around, and began to push him backward, moving slowly toward the blazing fireplace.

"In Heaven's name, Hannah! What in God's name are you doing?" Marmee cried out.

She and her daughters watched, in stunned silence, unable to comprehend and certainly unable to react quickly enough to help Father. Jo dropped the bottle of wine and the cup of beef tea, which shattered on the hardwood floor, as she let out a wild cry. Everyone watched as Hannah, her face set with grim determina-tion, struggled with Father. Faint, inhuman sounds issued from her throat as she forced him ever so slowly backward, closer to the fire. When the heel of his boot caught on a raised hearthstone, she pushed him away from her. Father tumbled backward and fell flat on his back onto the blazing logs. A bright shower of sparks corkscrewed up the chimney as the flames engulfed him with a roar.

What happened next would be the subject of great discussion for a long time afterward in the March household, but all agreed that something most unnatural occurred in their home for, indeed, it was evident that the figure they had assumed was Father was, indeed, not that personage at all. The flames quickly consumed the outer shell of the creature that had taken the shape of their loving husband and father, and writhing and thrashing about on the floor, it all the while emitted shrill, screeching sounds that reminded Jo of the cries a coyote makes in the forest on a full moon night. The skin of the being's face burned away with the hissing blue flare of a gas jet, peeling back skin to expose another visage hidden beneath, one that had scaled green skin like a frog's, large shining oval eyes the color of ebony, and three rows of needle-sharp teeth.

No one in the little parlor spoke or dared move until the figure finally stopped twitching, leaving naught but the charred bones of a most inhuman-looking skele-ton. Even these soon crumbled away to a fine, gray dust. The family exchanged unspoken glances as the most noxious fumes imaginable filled the air, choking them. Marmee, in stunned stupefaction because of what she and her children had just witnessed, shook herself and commanded Laurie, who was nearest to the door, to please open the door and allow some fresh air in.

Laurie did as he was told, and in the ensuing silence, all of them could hear and not deny what Beth was saying from her dark corner by the fireplace.

"I told you that wasn't Father at the door," she whispered. "Doesn't anybody ever listen to me?"

The Green Menace

By

Thomas Tessier

I was weeding one of the flower beds out front when the black Cadillac came up the gravel drive and stopped just a few feet away from me. With its hooded headlights and the two huge chrome bullets mounted on the wide grille, it looked like some giant mechanical land shark. At the time—this was in May of 1955—I thought it was one of the most beautiful cars I'd ever seen.

The man who got out of the Caddy dropped a cigarette to the ground and crushed it with his shoe. He was wearing a plaid flannel shirt, not tucked in, and khaki slacks. He didn't look like someone who spent a lot of time outdoors. The skin on his face was chalky and I could see that he had office hands. It was still the middle of the afternoon and he already had a shadow filling in along both sides of his jaw.

"Hey, kid," he said to me. "Give me a hand here."

I dropped the hoe I was working with and followed him around to the back of the car. He opened the trunk. There were two suitcases inside, one a little smaller than the other, as well as a black briefcase. He immediately grabbed the smaller suitcase and took that one himself.

"Get those other two for me, would you."

"Sure. How long are you staying?"

He ignored that, slammed the trunk shut, and stomped up the wooden steps to the veranda and through the front door, like he knew the place. Which he didn't; I was sure he'd never been to Sommerwynd before. Though I do remember thinking there was something vaguely familiar about him, like maybe I had seen his face on a baseball card a while back—not one of the keepsies.

My father was at the desk and quickly fell into conversation with the man as he signed in. I wasn't really paying attention, just standing there, waiting to find out which room he was given. But then my mother came out of the office, followed by my grandfather, and I saw the adoring look on their faces as my father introduced them. And then my father gestured toward me.

"And you have already met Kurt, our son. Kurt, this is our distinguished guest, Senator Joe McCarthy."

So that was why he looked familiar. I'd seen his face in a newspaper or on the television. But I was still a couple of months shy of sixteen at the time and had no interest at all in politics. The only thing I knew about him then was that he was a Commie-hunter and was loved for it by a lot of people, especially in our home state of Wisconsin. I nodded and mumbled something incoherent when McCarthy glanced at me and shook my hand. He had a so-so grip and cool, dry skin.

"Kurt," my father continued, "anything the Senator needs or wants while he is our guest, please see to it at once, or tell me or your mother."

"One thing," McCarthy said, raising a hand, his index finger extended. "I am here to get away from Washington and all that for a little while. So, I'd appreciate it if all of you would skip the 'Senator' stuff and just call me Joe." He looked at me again and gave a thin smile. "That includes you, kid—Kurt."

He was in room number 6, the best of the nine guest rooms at the lodge. It had the widest view of the lake, its own little balcony, and the largest bathroom. He kind of exhaled when he stepped inside and looked around, like he was not impressed. I heard an odd clunk when he set down the smaller suitcase he carried. He reached into his pants pocket, pulled out a money clip, and peeled off a dollar bill. He handed it to me.

"When you get a chance," he said, pointing to the coffee table in the sitting area, specifically to the clamshell ashtray on the table, "I'll need a bigger ashtray. And a bucket of ice."

"Yes, sir."

Knotty pine. He was surrounded by knotty pine, floor to ceiling on every wall, and it made him feel kind of edgy. Joe was fifteen minutes into his escape-from-the-rest-of-the-world, as he thought of it, and he was already wondering if he had made a mistake. Just one more in a long list of them, ha ha.

He was at Sommerwynd, a small fishing lodge on a small lake in a remote corner of northwestern Wisconsin. It didn't have a telephone, and the nearest town was twenty-odd miles away. It was the perfect place to go to ground for a while, to relax, recharge his batteries, and think about what he wanted to do next, to plan his next moves. If there were any. Billy O'Brien knew the Wirth family, who ran Sommerwynd. Billy had made the arrangements for Joe. Billy was a friend who stayed a friend—he didn't drift away, like so many others had. But now Billy had landed Joe out in the back of beyond, and Joe was not sure it was such a great idea after all. Still, give it a go. He could always leave whenever he felt like it.

Joe reached both hands behind him and up under his loose shirt to unhook the holster and the .22 clipped to his pants belt. He set them down on the bedside table. Then he pulled his left pant-leg up and unbuckled the holster and the snub-nosed .38 he wore above his ankle. He put them on the table next to the big armchair on the other side of the room. He'd never had to use either gun—yet. But Joe knew he had millions of enemies out there and he was not about to go down without a fight if any of them decided to come hunting for him.

He pulled the smaller suitcase close to the writing table, where he was sitting. He flipped the latches and carefully opened it on the floor. Inside, securely wrapped in cloth hand towels, were eight bottles of Jim Beam, along with Joe's favorite Waterford crystal whiskey tumbler. He put the drinking glass and one bottle of the bourbon on the desk, closed the suitcase, and set it down on the floor, right next to the night table beside the bed. He cracked open the bottle, poured a couple of fingers, and took a good sip. That helped. He lit a cigarette, then took another gulp of the whiskey, savoring the mixed flavors of bourbon and tobacco in his mouth. That's more like it, he thought, feeling a little better already.

I fetched a heavy glass ashtray from the supply cupboard and then went to the ice house, where I chipped off enough small chunks of ice to fill a large thermos. I wasn't expecting another tip, and didn't get one. He took the ice and the ashtray from me at the door of his room, muttered thanks and kicked the door shut with his foot.

I saw him again that first evening when he came down to the dining room for supper. The season at Sommerwynd didn't really start until after the Memorial Day weekend, so the only other guests were an older couple, the Gaults, who visited every year. McCarthy nodded politely to them when he entered the room, and then sat as far away from them as he could. He looked like a man with a lot on his mind—more than once I saw him wipe his hand down across his face and give a slight shake of the head, as if he were trying to change the subject of his thoughts.

My mother explained to me how McCarthy had been a kind of national hero, rousting out Reds who had infiltrated the American government, leading the fight to preserve the American way of life and protect our country from the threat within. But his enemies struck back and somehow managed to get the U.S. Senate to censure McCarthy in a vote the previous December. So that was what he had come to Sommerwynd to get away from.

At the time, I didn't understand much of it and I wasn't curious to learn more. I just nodded as my mother went on about what a good man McCarthy was and my father chimed in to say how gutless, shameful, and treasonous the Senate was in their action against him. I remember trying to translate it into baseball terms. He was like a pitcher who made it to the big leagues, a rising star, but then his opponents figured out how to hit him, and beat him. Guys like that— if they don't learn a new pitch or change their delivery, they don't often make it back to the top.

It was a nice evening to sit out on the front veranda or back patio, or for a stroll down to the boat dock, but McCarthy finished his meal, skipped dessert and coffee, and went back upstairs to his room. I did catch a glimpse of him a little while later, about the time when the frogs start up their chorus. I was taking the day's food scraps out to the compost heap near the vegetable beds. On my way back to the house, I saw him sitting at the table on the small balcony off his room. McCarthy didn't appear to notice me; he was probably just staring off at the view across the lake and the rising moon. I saw a curl of smoke in the dusk light, and a sudden glow from his cigarette as he inhaled.

The frogs were having a party, somewhere down the right shoreline some distance from the lodge. They began croaking and thrumming away even before the sun's descent reached the high tree line on the far side of the lake. At first, Joe didn't mind listening to them. It was the kind of nature sound you would expect to hear in a place like Sommerwynd—frogs croaking, owls hooting, bats flapping in the night air, a fish jumping and slapping back into the water. Sounds that felt right.

But after an hour and a half of it, Joe began to wish they would just shut up. "Come on, give it a rest, guys," he muttered as he poured another drink.

It amazed him how loud they were. The frogs didn't appear to be close to the lodge, their ribbity croaking seemed to come from a fair distance away—and yet, the volume they produced was quite strong. And the numbers of them. It didn't sound like a group of six or eight frogs, more like dozens and dozens of them. As darkness settled in for the night, their noise and numbers actually appeared to increase. Maybe the sound just carried very well in the deep stillness of the location, with the lake surrounded on all sides by forest.

Joe finally had enough of it and went inside, shutting the door to the balcony. He could still hear the frogs, but their sound was greatly diminished. He fixed another drink and pulled out *Triumph and Tragedy,* the final volume of Winston Churchill's history of the Second World War. He knew he would need something to occupy time like this at Sommerwynd, and he figured that Churchill was a good man to read when you were in a tough spot. He had already tried the radio in his room, but the only station he could pick up faded in and out of static—he caught a bit of a song that sounded like Patti Page being electrocuted.

Joe read for a while, then set the book aside. It was one of those moments— occurring more frequently of late—when he felt he had little or no patience left for anything. Not the book he was reading, not the room he was sitting in, not the building or place he was in, nobody he knew or encountered, not the weather, the season, the time of day or night. Nothing, not even himself.

He picked up one of his pistols and toyed idly with it in his hands. There was a certain comfort to be found in the kind of inanimate object that is simple in design and serves its purpose, and needs no other reason to be. A spoon, a fork, a knife, a shovel, a clay tile, a garden hose. A gun. Like this one. There had been moments in the past year when he was almost tempted to go that route. But his enemies would have loved it if he did, and he would never give them the satisfaction.

He could still hear the frogs. Jesus Christ, didn't they ever stop? It was a low throbbing sound, boombadaboombadaboom in an endless beat. Fat, slimy creatures rumbling in the muck. Joe undressed, crawled into bed, and turned off the table lamp. He quickly fell asleep, but drifted back up very close to consciousness some while later, again dimly aware of the frogs—still going at it.

Croak—you're croaked.

Croak—you're croaked.

Joe didn't turn on the light. In the darkness, he got out of bed, got a hold of his tumbler and the bottle of Jim Beam, poured one more large one, fumbled for a cigarette and the matches, and eased himself into the armchair. He did all this without opening his eyes, because to do so would make him more awake, and the whole point of getting up was to maintain this state of semi-consciousness, drifting along the edge of the one and the other, not quite awake or asleep. He knew without forming the thought that it would take two cigarettes to finish this drink. Then he would transport himself back to bed, and sleep would come again, and then it would finally hold.

Croak—you're croaked.

Joe made a kind of sighing, humming noise, not much more than a low, droning murmur within himself. It didn't sound like anything, but he knew what he meant by it. He meant: *Fuck you. Fuck all of you.*

McCarthy didn't come downstairs for breakfast the next morning. He did just make it in time for lunch, but all he wanted was coffee, and a lot of it. Mom brewed up a fresh pot for him and he drank most of it while sitting on the front veranda, one cup after another, each with its own cigarette.

I was nearby, working again on the flowerbeds, but I didn't say anything to him. It seemed pretty clear that he wanted to be left alone. He looked as washed-out and beat-down as anybody I'd ever seen. I tried not to keep glancing up at him, but it wasn't easy. Just knowing he was somebody important, or had been.

When he'd had enough coffee, McCarthy went back inside and I didn't see him for almost an hour. Then he came on the veranda again, this time with a little bounce in his step. He clattered down the front stairs and came over to me.

"Tell me something, kid," he said. "What's with those frogs?"

"You mean their croaking at night?"

"That's exactly what I mean. They kept me up all night."

He said it almost as if it was my fault, and his blue eyes bored into me like I knew something I wasn't telling him. Which I didn't.

"It's the time of year when they do that," I replied with a shrug. "It can be annoying at first, but you get used to it and don't even notice after a while."

"If they make that kind of racket every night, I won't be here long enough to get used to it." McCarthy started to step away, but then he turned back to me. "I'm going to go for a walk. Are there any good trails here, so I don't get lost?"

"Sure. There's one that goes all the way up to the top of that ridge," I said, pointing off to the rising tree line to the east. "There's a nice view at the top, and then the path circles down and around, back here to the lodge."

"Uphill," McCarthy said. "That sounds kind of strenuous."

"There's another trail that goes all the way around the lake," I told him. "It sticks pretty close to the water and it's mostly level ground."

"That sounds better."

I gave him directions to find the path—out behind the house, beyond the generator building, the boat dock, and my grandfather's workshop. McCarthy nodded his head and set off on his hike.

A little less than an hour later, I heard the gunshots.

Joe took note of his surroundings as he walked. It was an odd kind of place, Sommerwynd. The lodge itself was nice enough. The lake was small but picture-perfect, and had no other development on it. According to Billy, some well-connected and well-off people visited Sommerwynd from June through September, valuing it for its remoteness and natural setting. Free use of a canoe or rowboat, fishing, swimming, hiking. There was supposed to be a tennis court, though Joe hadn't seen it yet, and would not be interested anyhow. Still, he wondered how the Wirth family managed it all, with just the four of them there at present. But then he figured that they probably just hired a few temporary workers to help out in the busy months.

He passed the first cinderblock building, which had four large propane tanks attached, and he could hear the generator humming inside, providing the electricity that kept the lodge going. A little farther on, he found the second cinderblock building, also painted white. It had no windows. The kid had referred to it as his grandfather's workshop. In other words, Joe thought, that's where Grandpa goes to get away from his family for a while. Have a drink in peace, flip through the few issues of *Playboy* he had smuggled in, and remember what it was like back when.

He soon found the trail, and before long it swung in with the shoreline of the lake, so that the trees behind him cut off any view of the lodge, and he was alone in the woods. A fly or a bug of some kind buzzed him for a couple of seconds—he swatted at it and kept walking, and it went away. Joe thought, not for the first time in his life, that Nature is overrated.

The path hugged the water for a good stretch, and there were a couple of times when Joe spotted small fish in the shallows. That was nice. Then, maybe a half hour into his hike, he came to a spot where the trail swung to the right, away from the lake and into the woods. He stood on a large flat rock that sat at the edge of the water and he studied the scene for a moment. He figured it out. A stream entered the lake here, but over time enough silt had accumulated to back up some of the flow, which created a small, swampy lagoon. The path went inland to get around this obstacle.

Joe was about to continue his walk, but then didn't. The lagoon itself was kind of pretty. It was too early for lily pads, but the glassy black water was already laced with duckweed. The rock he was standing on was in the shade, making this a good spot to take a break. He pulled the hip flask out of his back pocket and sat down on the rock, his feet dangling a few inches off the ground. A sip, a cigarette. There was a cool breeze coming off the lake, and he sat facing into it, enjoying the way it felt on his skin, the way it rippled the water. Yeah, Nature was overrated, but it did have its moments.

Part of him wanted to go back to DC and resume the battle. Or restart it, more accurately. But another part of him said that the battle was over, finished, and that he had lost it. Forget it, move on. But move on to what? What was left? For a while, it was as if the whole world watched him and listened to him—how do you get that back? Because now, he was invisible.

An odd sensation crept over him, that he was not alone. He turned around, wondering if someone from the lodge had come with a message, but there was no one on the trail. Then Joe looked at the lagoon—and he saw a pair of eyes in the water. Dozens of pairs of eyes, just breaking the surface, looking at him. It startled him, but he quickly realized that this lagoon was where those noisy frogs lived, and there they were, looking at him. The lagoon was full of them, more than he could count.

Joe stood up, flicked his cigarette into the water, and stepped down off the rock. A few feet away, a frog crawled forward, partly out of the water. It was huge, the size of a watermelon. *Jesus.* Joe looked around, spotted a pebble, picked it up and flung it into the lagoon. It splashed close to one frog, but the creature didn't move. A couple of frogs had emerged from the lagoon and were now crawl-hopping toward him. Joe pulled his right foot back and kicked one of them back into the water. The frog was so heavy that Joe felt the strain in his ankle muscles. The frog flopped backward, just a couple of yards away, righted itself, and began to move forward again. The other frog, now on the ground, jumped and caught Joe's ankle in its mouth. Teeth, the damned thing had teeth! Joe tried to shake it off, but the frog held on. Joe raised his other foot and slammed it as hard as he could down on the frog's head.

Nothing—that was what he got for wearing sneakers in the woods. And that was when he noticed that the frog had whiskers around its mouth, which shot out like small blades, one of them piercing Joe's calf. What kind of frogs were these, that had teeth and sharp barbels like a catfish?

Think about that later. The pain began to hit him. Joe reached behind his back, got his .22 out, held it to the side of the frog's head and squeezed the trigger. Blood and flesh flew, and the frog at last dropped off his ankle. But Joe was astonished to see that other frogs were coming forward, at him. Calmly, he aimed the pistol and shot them in the head or face, until the gun was empty. He had a couple of boxes of bullets back at the lodge. He reached down to get the .38 from his good ankle, and proceeded to empty that into another bunch of frogs as they got closer to him.

Then, he knew it was time to leave. Joe grabbed one of the dead frogs by the leg and hurried away with it, back to the lodge.

Well, we'd seen these frogs, of course, and thought nothing of them. They never bothered us and we never bothered them. My grandfather, Klaus Wirth, claimed to have refined some of their unusual features through cross-breeding. He was a biologist, a great admirer of Luther Burbank. He had returned to Germany in the 1920s to continue his research work. He was not a Nazi, but after Hitler came to power he was not allowed to leave the country, and was pressed into government scientific service. In my family, none of us ever seemed to know quite what that meant. In any event, my grandfather returned to Wisconsin after the war, refused to seek work at any university, and declared himself in retirement. Still, he conducted what he called "research." He and my father converted the old chicken coop into what became my grandfather's workshop. We knew that he had scientific equipment, and animals imported—even that he had obtained frogs from Africa, with teeth. Still, whenever my grandfather hinted at a "breakthrough," my mother and father rolled their eyes.

Now we had Senator Joseph McCarthy sitting on the patio, one bare foot propped up on a chair, my mother carefully wiping his wounds with disinfectant, me and my father standing nearby, not knowing what to say. My grandfather hung back a couple of yards from the rest of us, looking as if he hoped that this would all blow over and he wouldn't have to move to Argentina.

And on the flagstone, a dead frog. With half of its head blown off. With nasty-looking teeth and whiskers. I'd seen them, but never one close up. It was very big, green and black, and it looked heavy, although I didn't try to lift it. The animal was so slimy and ugly, I wanted nothing to do with it.

My parents were endlessly apologetic, but McCarthy kept going on and on, asking questions they couldn't answer, suggesting that there was some actual plot or plan in place—yes, there, in the middle of nowhere in northern Wisconsin—to somehow create a vicious creature that would eventually wreak havoc on the land.

"This is the goddamn *uber*-frog," McCarthy shouted.

At that point I actually reached down and ran my fingers along the teeth in the open mouth of the dead frog. They were not large, but felt very sharp. I stood up and backed away, wiping my fingers on my pants. My grandfather gave me a little nod of the head and I stepped back to see what he wanted. He whispered in my ear.

"They eat fish and bugs, nothing more, that I know of." Then he added, "They grow too quickly, this new stage."

My mother had McCarthy's leg all cleaned and wrapped by then, and he did seem to be a little more composed. Still, he glanced at my grandfather and said, "I'd like to take a look at that workshop of yours, Pops."

My grandfather suddenly turned icy—something I cannot remember ever seeing until that moment. His eyes narrowed and he spoke quietly through a slight smile.

"I do not believe you have security clearance for that."

McCarthy did a little double-take at that, but before he could come up with a response, a woman screamed. I knew right away it was Mrs. Gault, since she and her husband were the only two people not on the patio. Sure enough, the Gaults came around one of the hedges screening off the generator building, Mrs. Gault limping, sobbing, and assisted by her husband.

"She's been attacked," he said. "By a frog!"

"They're coming," Mrs. Gault wailed.

"Masses of them," her husband added.

I took off while he was rambling on. I ran down across the lawn, around the line of hemlocks, past the generator building, and then I saw them. They hadn't reached my grandfather's workshop yet, but they were closing in. Hundreds of huge frogs, hopping fitfully through the tall grass—toward the lodge, us. I turned around, ran back to the patio, and told my father what I'd seen. He just kind of went into a distant stare for a few moments.

My mother, who was already wiping and dressing Mrs. Gault's ankle-bite, said, "Perhaps we should all go inside."

"Or just leave," Mr. Gault snarled.

That was when McCarthy raised his hand and wagged his fingers at me. I went over to him. He pulled a key out his pocket and handed it to me.

"In my room, in the large suitcase, there's a couple of boxes of bullets. Go get them for me. Quick!"

Looking back, I was caught up in it. I flew.

The lodgekeeper, Karl Wirth, looked frozen, but Joe knew what had to be done. They could run like rats, or they could stop this in its tracks. It wasn't really a choice.

"Do you have any guns?" Joe asked.

"A rifle, a shotgun," Wirth replied.

"That's it?"

"Yes."

"I thought this was a hunting lodge."

"Fishing, swimming, boating," Wirth said. "A bit of hunting in season, but that's for the guests. They bring their own rifles. I'm not a hunter myself."

"Get them," Joe ordered. "And all the ammo you've got."

Wirth hurried away obediently. Joe told Mrs. Wirth and the Gaults to go inside the lodge. He walked out on the lawn, toward the lake. His leg throbbed, but the pain was not unbearable. He was a little past the generator building when he spotted them, a black and green wave surging forward. Ugly bastards. Oh yes, he'd put a stir in them, no doubt about it. But it was inevitable. These people, the Wirths, were living in a dream—oh, we don't bother them, they don't bother us. Just drifting along, until the time came when it was too late, and the moment became one of *their* choosing, not yours.

The kid was back, with the bullets. "Ever use one of these?" Joe asked, handing Kurt the .22.

"I did target shooting a couple of times."

"Good enough. Load up, and aim for the ones in front. Take your time, they're not exactly fast on the ground."

Joe led the way and when they got to the old man's workshop, they began plunking frogs along the advancing front line. It shook him, how many there were of the beasts. He knew then that they didn't have nearly enough bullets. At some point, they would have no alternative but to run for their cars and flee. But Joe noticed that as he and the kid moved laterally, so did the frogs. Vicious, but very dumb creatures. Where could he lead them?

I admit, I was into it. Maybe because it didn't seem to be that dangerous a threat, really. We always had the option of leaving, and coming back later with some kind of professional or state help to eradicate the frogs—or whatever would be done with them. But I got a kick out of picking them off, one at a time, seeing their fat bodies pop in blood and pus. It was like, suddenly you're in a movie, and you're playing this part, and it's more fun than what you'd normally be doing at that time of day.

Unfortunately, we ran out of bullets fast, and there were *a lot* of frogs still coming. My father arrived then, with his rifle and shotgun and a couple of boxes of cartridges. McCarthy grabbed the rifle and started snapping in shells. He moved us away from the direction of the house, and the frogs followed, coming after us—I thought that was so smart of him, but I didn't know what good it would do. McCarthy directed my father's fire, a shotgun blast here, there, almost as if he were steering the flow of the frogs as they came at us. Whenever one edge of the wave appeared to be moving closer, McCarthy fired a couple of shots himself, picking off frogs that he took to be leaders in the throng.

We got to the generator building, and the frogs had come around both sides of my grandfather's workshop. My father and I stood there, waiting for McCarthy to say or do something, but he was standing there, letting the frogs get closer and closer. Finally, he turned to me.

"You run that way around the building, back to the lodge," he said. "If they start getting close, pack everybody in the cars and get out." He turned to my father and said the same thing, except that he pointed my father in the other direction around the building. He slapped us both on the back. "Go!"

"Wait," I said. "What are you going to do?"

"Just gonna let them get a little closer and make sure they're coming on both sides, then I'll be right behind you."

Except that he wasn't right behind us. My father and I met up on the patio, and moved out into the driveway area on the other side of the hedges so that we could see what was happening. We saw the frogs closing in on the generator building, and then McCarthy scrambled out on the side away from the house, running toward the edge of the woods. He was limping, but made good time. The frogs were coming around both sides of the generator building, toward the house. Some peeled off, to go after McCarthy. He dived into the brush at the edge of the tree line, and a moment later, rifle shots rang out. I was slow when it came to following his line of thought, but it became clear a few seconds later when he hit one of the propane tanks, and it went off, and the others followed almost immediately. *Whoomph! Whoomph-whoom-whoom-whoomph!*

It took me years to decipher the visual images I have in my head. Yes, the fireball dominated, but eventually I began to see that a flat sheet of flame also spread out at the same time. Lower to the ground. It was lost for a time—I kept seeing sheet metal fly off the roof, cinderblocks blasted into chunks. We stood there for a long time while the smoke and dust and debris settled. Then we could see a lot of scorched frogs, dead on the ground, and I spotted a few others still alive, retreating toward the lagoon.

Son of a bitch, it worked. Joe stood up and walked toward the house. He looked all around, but couldn't see a live frog that wasn't heading the other way. It would do for now, but the problem remained, and would have to be dealt with.

He found the kid and his father on the patio, both looking shell-shocked, though the kid had a smile lurking on the edges of his mouth. Joe liked that, and slapped the kid on the back.

"You did good."

"Thanks!"

Joe turned to the father, was it Karl or Klaus? He wasn't sure, but it didn't matter. The guy was just standing there, hoping that normal life would somehow be restored to him. Joe smiled reassuringly.

"You've got insurance, right?"

It took a few seconds, but then the man nodded.

"Ah, good, you'll be fine then."

Joe went inside, packed his things, came downstairs, and tried to check out. Mrs. Wirth wouldn't let him pay a cent. She was very apologetic, as was Joe. The lodge had no electricity now, so everyone was preparing to move out until repair work could be arranged and carried out.

"Just a thought," Joe said before he left. "I wouldn't try to explain this in too much detail. An accidental explosion is an accidental explosion."

Tell her husband the same thing, and he probably wouldn't get it, but Mrs. Wirth nodded immediately. When Joe was turning away from the front desk, he saw the kid crossing the other side of the lobby.

"Kurt, would you grab a couple of these bags for me?"

We got over it. We spent a few days at our winter house 40 miles away while Dad got the insurance and repair stuff taken care of, and the investigation went the usual path of least resistance. An accident is an accident, there was no question of gain in the case. And we went back, and had a good season. The new generator was a beauty and actually saved money.

My grandfather never went back to his workshop. When he died a couple of years later, some people came in and took away his equipment, and my parents just let the empty building rot. As was always the case in my family, when there was no need to talk about something, we didn't.

I've learned a lot about McCarthy since then, and it's hard to find anything in it that I like. I think he grew up at a time and in a place where he learned that if you didn't beat up the other guy, he'd beat up you, and he lived accordingly. I know what it's like to grow up feeling alone. When I heard a year or so later that McCarthy had died in a hospital, that he was an alcoholic and had struggled with all kinds of health issues, I thought it was a very sad end to an important life. Later, after I got to know more about him, I came to think that it was just a sad end to a life. He was not a likeable man, but I have to say that I kind of liked him at the time.

My father died of a heart attack a few years later. My mother had to sell Sommerwynd. For a long time nothing much happened out there, but there are a lot of very expensive summer homes on that lake now.

The frogs? The state killed them off, as an invasive species. At least, I think they killed them all off. I don't live there anymore. I'm in sales, in Madison. No wife, no kids, not sure how I ended up here. But I'm doing okay.

Still a long drive ahead. Joe decided to kill it now. He pulled into a place called The Valley Inn while the sun was still visible in the sky. A string of bungalows in the middle of nowhere, on the road to nowhere. Let's say nothing about the room, but that it had a television and got two snowy channels. He poured a couple of fingers of Jim Beam into a plastic cup, and lit a Pall Mall.

Might as well have done this in the first place.

Benediction

By

Tom Piccirilli

The Ganooch raised a withered hand and aimed a skeletal finger at me. His breathing came in ragged gasps and he could barely manage to hiss out my name.

I pressed my way through his gathered family, went to my knee beside his bed, and said, "I'm here, Frankie."

His slack mouth tried to frame words, but nothing came out. I huddled closer and put my ear to his lips. As he breathed through his teeth the delicate wisps of his white stringy hair blew across my cheek. His skin was so thin now that it had split along the seams and wrinkles of his face, leaving his crows' feet crusted with dried blood.

Don Franco Ganucci was forty-seven years old and looked like he was well past ninety. Eight days ago we'd played three games of racquetball together and then gone out to dinner at Ventimiglio's, where the Ganooch picked up the best-looking girl in the place. He always got the best-looking girl in every place we went because he was handsome, slender, fit, exuded real presence, and nearly as rich as an Arabian prince.

His eyes focused on me. They were so bloodshot I couldn't even tell what color they were anymore. He sucked air like a dying fish.

"Protect ... *la* ... *famiglia*," he said, raising his right hand up a few inches.

I took it and said, "I promise, Frankie."

I hoped to Christ that whatever he had wasn't contagious.

One set of doctors said it was an ultra-aggressive form of cancer. Another told us it was some kind of radiation poisoning. The young priests called it the will of God. The old nuns suspected demonic attack.

Ganooch gurgled out one final breath and then finally let go.

Grandma Ganucci began to wail and hurl herself across the room, calling down all the saints. The rest of the clan tried to calm her but she went two-forty of stocky muscle and broke free easy. Her rosary whipped around her like a single engine motor. She could snap the neck of a lion with those arms. For fifty years she'd been getting up at dawn to cook for the family, the consigliere, the account-ants, the capos, all the legbreakers, the hitters, the torpedoes, stirring pots of sauce and making fresh cannoli and zeppoles every day. She ran through the family and knocked them around, her howls and wails shaking the reinforced glass in the window frames.

Cole Portman, Ganooch's consigliere, turned to me with his stoic features almost showing a touch of emotion. He whispered, "You think it was a hit?"

"Yes," I said.

"Who kills a man this way?"

"I don't know."

"The Jamaicans? The Haitians? They use poisons."

I shook my head. "Nothing that does this to a man."

"The Russian mob? You remember that story about the spy who was murdered slowly with radiation?"

I didn't answer. I watched the family in their grief. Helen, the Ganooch's wife, looked like she was hardwired to the third rail. Current seemed to be running through her as she shook and sort of danced in place. Gina, his daughter, was trying to hold herself together while she stared at her dead father's decrepit corpse. She glanced at me once and our eyes met. She was twenty and dark and beautiful and her sorrow made me want her even more. We'd been lovers for two months and had yet to share so much as a romantic dinner. We met in the deep night when the family was asleep and the estate guards were prowling the grounds. I made the effort to give her all my sympathy in the glance we shared. I didn't have much to begin with, but what I had I wanted to give to her.

The Ganooch's nineteen-year-old son, Tommy, made the effort of holding his mother tightly and hugging her to his chest while she sobbed. She flapped her forearms weakly around him and eventually sank to her knees. He went down along with her, his pretty-boy face brimming with confusion. He was head of the family now and the knowledge of it made his eyes practically swirl.

Portman leaned in to me and said, "Some of the capos are showing signs of jumping ship. Pastore will start wooing them. He knows we're weak now."

"They won't leave."

He nodded. He knew our men were all afraid of me. They'd seen me up close in action. They still feared blades and bullets more than a mysterious week-long terminal disease. The politics of the syndicate was making everybody nervous.

But the Ganooch was just going to be the first. I could feel it. Next in line for the throne was Tommy, if we stuck to tradition. But nobody would. Instead, Chaz Argento, the Ganooch's senior capo, would take the reins. There might be some grumbles. There might some in-fighting, captains crashing other territories, crews trying to make it on their own. These things had a way of boiling over and then settling down on their own.

The heads of the other families would throw a big customary celebration full of the usual syndicate nonsense, and Chaz would come out the frontrunner and kiss the capos on their cheeks and immediately buy a new house twice as big as his old one and start living larger than he ever had before.

I wondered if Chaz could've gotten his hands on some kind of radiation or poison. I knew Chaz as well as any of us could know each other in this life. He had been a loyal second to Frankie Ganucci. They'd come up together on the same street in Brooklyn and were best friends. It didn't mean Chaz couldn't have clipped the don, but I had serious doubts.

"I'm putting you in charge of this," Portman said. "Find whoever has done this. Protect the family."

"I've already made that promise."

"I'm calling together a meeting of the captains this afternoon."

"I thought you might."

He stared at me hard. He had to be wondering if I had slipped something to Frankie, but you had to trust someone and trusting your torpedo was as good a bet as you could get. "Where are you going to start?" he asked. "With Argento?"

I knew death. I'd been doing this for a long time. I made a study of it. I practiced at it. I learned from the street, and I learned from the best. I learned from men who'd done their tours in a land of dust that hadn't seen peace for ten thousand years. I knew death. And no man aged fifty years in a week. There was no cancer this aggressive. There was no known infection or toxin that could do this. I thought of the young priests calling this the will of God. They were wrong.

"With the nuns," I said.

Like just about everyone in our business, in Brooklyn anyway, I was a Catholic who still went to mass every Sunday. I knew the names of all the priests, gave generously to my local diocese, and took communion. Even though syndicate members tended to edit out some of our more nefarious deeds in the confessional, we all thought of ourselves as good Catholics. Don Ganucci used to be an altar boy. So had Argento. So had I.

Unlike the others, though, I used to suffer from spells and visions as a kid. My old man, who was a second-string boxer who couldn't keep off the H, used to slug me and my mother around a lot. I used to wonder, while she nursed me through the horrible headaches, her own nose broken, sometimes bleeding from her ear, if he was doing real damage to us. Until I hit puberty I used to have insane hallucinations of angels clinging to the high corners of my bedroom, staring down with judgment and disappointment, aiming fiery swords at my heart. I used to sleepwalk and sometimes wake to find myself standing over my father's bed with a kitchen knife in my hand, poised at the thick stubble of his throat.

I walked to the front gate where three family soldiers stood inside a huge security booth of bulletproof glass. I signaled for them to let me out. Instead they opened the booth door and gave me a hard time about hitting the street alone. They were strapped to the teeth. Portman had already put the word out that the Ganooch had been iced. The foot soldiers wanted to chauffeur me in one of the Lincoln stretch limos, but I wanted to stroll the neighborhood and prepare myself. They didn't argue with me that much. No one ever did.

I wandered the streets where I'd grown up. They were the same as they had been twenty years ago, with the same privately owned shops standing side by side. There were still fruit carts on the corner. There was still a man who would come and sharpen your knives. No draw-down metal shutters were necessary. There was no sign of yuppie influx or any kind of conglomerate takeover of the small stores.

The Ganooch and his father, Don Rafael, had refused to let the corporate sinkholes lay any claim to roughly four square blocks of the neighborhood. In this age that was considered a minor miracle. The locals would line up by the hundreds at Frankie's funeral, same as they had for the old don. I waved to Mr. Palazzolo, the butcher, and Mr. and Mrs. Iacobuzio, the grocers. And Joey the T, and Frankie Sabia and his brother Jocko. And Paulie the Lemon Squeeze, and Eddie the Ear. And Mrs. Aspetta, ninety-two and hosing off the sidewalk in front of her furniture shop. They knew who I was and what I did, but they called to me and waved, and it wasn't out of fear. They knew they were under my protection. There wasn't any one of them that would've denied me anything.

I turned the corner and could see the spire of St. Mark's church in the distance. To one end of the block was the rectory and the seminary, and to the other was St. Anne's, the Catholic school I'd graduated from. Across the street was the convent.

I put a little more step in my stride and cut through the alleys and turned the corner of the schoolyard where kids were playing out on the playground. Sister Christina May was out there behind home plate umpiring, her habit flapping in the breeze.

I glanced up at the fourth floor of the convent.

There was one nun who spooked everyone in Brooklyn. The priests, the archdiocese, the Mother Superior, the rest of the sisters. Hell, maybe even the Pope for all I knew. In another time they would've put her away in a mental institution, or at least turned a hand toward exorcism, but as things stood we had somehow entered a more devout yet solemn age of reason, so they left her mostly alone on the fourth floor in a suite of small rooms filled with crucifixes and pictures of the blessed heart.

I walked into the building. The convent had its hardened troops too, same as any syndicate family. An elderly sister I recalled being a geometry teacher when I was a kid had taken up station at the front desk. I stepped up and gave her my warmest smile. She returned it, reached for my hand, took it in a powerful grip.

"Hello, I'm Sister Maeve. How may I help you?"

"I'd like to see Sister Abigail," I said.

Her face closed up like a fist, with a not-so-subtle spark of fear flashing in her eyes, just the way I knew it would happen. "Sister Abigail doesn't receive visitors."

"She'll receive me."

"No, I'm afraid you don't understand. You see, she—"

"I understand perfectly."

"Who shall I say is calling?"

"Her son."

"Oh." She turned away from me and I wondered if she might cross herself. She didn't. "It's you. I remember you now."

"Yes."

She picked up the phone but I knew my mother didn't have a phone in her room. Sister Maeve was calling the Mother Superior, who had once taught physics classes. She was a realist. Anyone running a convent in Brooklyn would have to be. She'd made her deals with the devil before.

"Please take a seat. Someone will be with you directly."

"Thank you."

I sat and stared at the Catholic iconography all around, the tortured faces, the twisted bodies, the loving eyes. They were the same as the ones in my mother's room. Martyrs glared at me from every corner. They looked no less angry than my father.

My old man had been a punch-drunk boxer with a weakness for heroin, whiskey, loud women, and a tendency toward self-pity. At the time my mother was an infrequent recreational drug user who began to get more and more stoned whenever my father went on a binge. She suffered from high fevers that sometimes drove her from the house in the middle of the night. Sometimes she'd be gone for days. My old man would eventually send me out to look for her in the alleys, crack dens, shooting galleries, whorehouses, and under the boardwalk at Coney Island. Wherever I found her she'd be babbling about the same angels I occasionally saw in my spells. We were two of a kind.

They used to fight like hell. Physically brawling. My mother had learned a lot from him over the years. How to duck, bob and weave, dodge wild swings, work his glass jaw. Neither one of them would be feeling any pain. The fights could last for a half hour or better. My mother would be seized by the power of speaking in tongues and start raving at him in an unknown language. He'd eventually get tuckered out and go sleep at one of his girlfriends' apartments.

Then my father took his final dive and lost most of the sight in his right eye. He was out of the ring but it didn't stop him from farming himself out as a Ganucci legbreaker. When I was fifteen I heard he tried to strongarm a couple of Jamaicans into sharing some of their turf and the cops found him the next morning with a butcher knife in his back, about a block away from our house.

While my mother was dressing for his funeral, the worst fever to ever afflict her struck. I watched her eyes roll back in her head and listened to her speak in tongues and thrash across the floor. Every time I tried to go for the phone an ancient voice full of desert dust told me to stay where I was. I stayed. She twisted and contorted and howled like a dog. Her eyes and ears bled. When it was over, I called an ambulance and she was in the hospital for a week of tests that never showed a damn thing and couldn't be paid for anyway.

The day she was released she became a nun, devoted herself to God, and became someone else's problem. I was sixteen and went to work for Don Rafael that afternoon. By the time I was twenty I was his number-one torpedo.

A door slammed somewhere deep in the building and the echo snapped off the corridor walls and thrummed in my chest. Severe-sounding footsteps followed. I knew the rhythm of that gait anywhere.

It took a full minute before Mother Superior turned a corner and, without expression, approached me. Sister Maeve ducked her head and pretended to be busy with paperwork.

Mother Superior didn't offer her hand and I didn't offer mine. We had a long and complex relationship. She used to beat the hell out of me with a yardstick. She used to keep me after school explaining I was smart enough to go to college and get far away from Brooklyn. She would come to me when the church ran into its various travails with the media. I had gotten reporters to retract stories. I had gotten witnesses in cases against priests to alter their testimonies. About five years ago a Chinese street gang was trying to establish a foothold in our area and set up distribution near St. Anne's, getting the kids hooked and starting them off as runners and movers for them. When Mother Superior found out she put in a call to me and I got in charge with the triads, who cleared up the problem without anyone else having to get directly involved.

Mother Superior would never admit it, but she needed me, on occasion.

Her face was bloated, stern, and craggy. If I'd ever seen her smile, I didn't remember it. She met my gaze directly and said, "Walk with me."

I did. We wandered the halls seemingly without direction. It didn't much matter where you went here. Every hall felt the same, every room showing no real personality besides the church's own. A thousand Christs, ten thousand crosses, St. Francis calling the animals, and more animals and more animals. I didn't understand how any of them shouldered the weight of two thousand years of blind dogma and history.

"Your mother has been worse of late."

"In what way?" I asked.

"Her nightmares have returned. The visions. She sometimes screams in the middle of the night."

"You should have sent her up to the Bronx psych center when you had the chance."

"You know I couldn't do that. She's not crazy."

I grunted. "How close an eye do you keep on her?"

"She's in the near-constant care of Sister Katherine and Sister Ruth Joyce."

I didn't know either of them. They must have been two of the younger nuns who were being tested in their own way.

"I need to see her."

At one time Mother Superior used to read me the riot act, make me promise to not upset my mother, not make her exert herself, not discuss certain topics with her. But she knew now that if I was here there had to be a dark reason for it. I didn't come around to bring cookies or flowers. I didn't show up for the neighborhood church basketball games or the street feasts or talent shows and choir rehearsals. I came when I was called, and I was never called for any sweet pretext.

We reached the sprawling staircase. I put my hand on the gray railing and could feel all the years of the convent trapped beneath the layers of paint like muted cries. I snatched my hand back like I'd been burned.

"Do you want me to take you up?" she asked.

"No."

"She can be quite ... taxing."

"I know."

She turned her austere features from me, possibly out of courtesy. She had questions. Everyone had questions. She was a good woman. She thought I still had a soul to save.

I took the stairs alone. I walked up to the fourth floor and could feel my pulse beginning to speed up. I took a minute to calm myself but it didn't help. I knocked at my mother's door and a young pretty nun appeared. Behind her, seated and reading the Bible, was another young woman with thick glasses and deep acne pits. Sister Katherine and Sister Ruth Joyce. They knew who I was. I told them I wanted to speak to my mother alone. They nodded and left.

My mother sat in the corner of the main room of her suite, near the window, but facing the wall. The sunshine lit up her back and the black garments seemed to drain the light away.

"Hello, Ma."

She glanced up at me, and for an instant I almost saw her the way she was before the old man had started to beat her and the darkness had fully gotten hold of her. She smiled in that easy way she had once always had about her. She'd at one time been comprised of a great grace and calm even when serious troubles were hitting. Now her eyes held a hint of amusement.

A strange tightness filled my chest. It might have been sorrow or regret. I had a catalogue of laments stacked up behind my heart. I wanted to drop to my knees and hug her. I had twenty years of tears dammed up.

"I wasn't sure if I'd ever see you again," she said.

"Can't get rid of a bad thing."

"You're not a bad thing."

I grinned. My grin made some men fall to pieces and drop to their knees. My mother merely smiled back. Her smile made priests cross themselves.

"Oh, I know," she continued, "that you've murdered. But have you ever hurt an innocent?"

"Nobody's innocent, Ma."

But I knew what she meant, and she was right, though that didn't absolve me in the eyes of God or even in my own. I'd never hurt anyone who wasn't already in the bent life, on a mob payroll, playing the syndicate game, or out to make the streets run red. It didn't make me a good man.

I could see that she hadn't been sleeping. Dark circles framed her eyes. She sat wearily, her face haggard, fatigue written into her features. I took her hand and she smiled again briefly. I sat beside her and she tightened her grip. It was almost enough to make me flinch. My mother didn't have an ounce of fat on her. She had real power.

"What have you been dreaming?" I asked.

"The same as you, son."

It was true that over the past couple of weeks I'd awoken from nightmares, sweating and groaning, unfamiliar words trapped in my throat. But I couldn't remember my dreams anymore. And I was certain that my mother could still recall her own.

"Who is it, Ma? Who killed Frankie? Some of the other nuns, they're talking about—" I couldn't make myself say the words. Demonic intervention. Satanic influence.

"I know what they're talking about," she said.

Her gaze tilted aside. She was looking into the places where no one could see without giving up a large part of themselves. Sweat dappled her forehead and ran down the creases that outlined her mouth. Heat emanated from her, and like flames passed from treetop to treetop, her fever set fire to mine.

Within seconds my scalp prickled and I had to undo my tie and take off my jacket. Sweat slithered across my chest and threaded down my back. I watched the pulse in her neck snap against the cowl.

She began to whisper prayers and blessings. I knew them well, and a part of me wanted to recite along with her. I had to force myself to keep from doing it, but the words grew louder and louder inside my head. My mother took my hand and pressed it to the side of her face. I wondered how we had ended up this way. It had something to do with my father. Something to do with our heritage. We'd been blessed and cursed and forgotten by God. She forced her head down and drew my palm across her eyes.

Images flashed in my mind. It was a familiar feeling even though this hadn't happened to me since I was fifteen. I watched light break upon the darkness. Blood splashing upon a tree. A beautiful curvaceous blonde woman without a face, who wasn't a woman. A strange black bug bouncing inside a glass jar. My mother's prayers became something else. Her words twisted and grew less decipherable. The language was no longer English. It wasn't Latin. It wasn't Greek. It might not have been human. I watched her and could feel the fever burning her alive, and I began to hiss out against God.

Whatever she was doing, whatever was happening to her, it had an effect on everything else around us. A gathering of crows flapped their dark wings against the windows. Screams of children from the schoolyard next door took a more vicious turn, as if they were killing each other. The temperature dropped. Our breath frosted in the air. Still we burned. The room dimmed. Clouds covered the sun. A few drops of rain spattered against the glass.

I glanced around at the Catholic iconography around me and could feel the eyes of the saints and martyrs, of Christ and his mother, of the cardinals and the bishop, of the Pope, staring sorrowfully with forlorn hearts.

My mother's mouth was full of tongues. She spat and growled and then there were many voices rising from her. I'd lived through this before as a boy. Like then, I tried to focus on what they were saying, what they wanted from her as well as from me.

I spoke to them, "What are you saying? What are you trying to tell me? I'm here, I'm listening, just spit it out, damn it."

The din continued. In the midst of the noise I could hear my mother arguing with other voices. She sounded strong and competent. I heard my name mentioned. The argument continued and I couldn't be certain if she was winning or losing. She seemed to be giving it her all. So did the others packed into her, whoever they were, whatever they wanted. I thought maybe I heard my father there for a moment. My name was a curse. They choked on it like broken glass.

I took her palm and kissed it.

And then the spell was over.

The heat dissipated. Sweat cooled on my face and the crows flew on. The children's screaming sounded less like killing and torture and more like kids squabbling over who was next up at kickball.

"There is a will at work," my mother said.

"Whose will?" I asked.

"*Pythoness.*"

"What?"

"*Fishwives.*"

The words rang bells from my altar boy days but I didn't remember why at the moment. "I don't understand."

"*Familiar spirit.*"

I shook my head. "What do I have to do, Ma?"

She came out of her trance in an instant, her eyes clearing. "I can't tell you that. You'll find your course. The same as you always have."

Then she slumped forward in her seat and nearly hit the floor. I caught her in my arms and carried her to her bed. I laid her on the mattress and sat beside her, watching her sleep for a while. She deserved better than having been married to my old man. She deserved better than being married now to Christ. She certainly deserved better than having me for a son.

I got up, straightened my tie, and put on my suit jacket. Distant thunder rumbled the walls. The blessed heart pictures all seemed to clatter in time together, beating to a particular rhythm. I walked out the door and Sister Katherine and Sister Ruth Joyce bid me good day and returned to my mother's side.

Cole Portman called together the capos to thrash out family business. Six of them along with members of their separate crews sat with Portman in the back room of the antique furniture warehouse that fronted some Ganucci bookmaking and drug-running. Someone had brought zeppoles and cannoli, and they sucked them down along with a couple of bottles of wine.

Chaz Argento had really gotten his shine on. He had a fresh haircut, a four-thousand-dollar suit on, and smelled of expensive cologne. I stood at the window staring at the last remnants of my mother's storm being carried east.

"Tommy has only had limited experience with the Ganucci trade," Portman said. "Running a few errands for his father here and there. The kid's a freshman at Brown, for Christ's sake. So let's not waste time discussing the option of whether he's in or out. He's not a serious contender for the business."

Everyone around the table nodded and agreed. I wondered if Frankie would have been pleased that they were cutting his kid out or if he would've gone ballistic that they weren't even considering his blood to head the family now. For the first time in fifty years a Ganucci wouldn't be running the show.

"So who becomes the skipper?" someone asked.

Chaz's legbreakers chuckled to themselves. Chaz couldn't contain his smile. He turned it on, full wattage. He touched the double Windsor knot of his tie and made sure it was perfect. He started to climb to his feet.

"I do," I said.

Portman groaned under his breath. Chaz looked like he'd just been tasered. His eyes got wide and his body began to tremble, and it seemed as if ten thousand watts were going through his brain. His boys jumped up and took two steps toward me. The rest began to argue and shout and rush around the room, strongarms holding back their captains, legbreakers unsure of how far they should go now. Wine spilled. The cannoli hit the floor. I turned back to the window. Someone snarled that they had never trusted me. Whoever it was was the smartest guy in the room.

Chaz's voice sliced through the rest of the noise. "I'm next in line. You think I've paid my way up the chain since I was ten years old, stealing soda cans and beer bottles out of old man Diego's market, just so that someone can cut me out now? You know how much I've earned for this family over the years?"

"Nobody's cutting you out, Chaz," I said.

"Damn right! And you, how do we know it wasn't you who clipped Frankie? You think we don't know you've been shacking with his daughter? This how you make your move?"

There were some murmurs at that. Apparently not everyone knew about me and Gina. There was some eye-rolling. There were glances of castigation. Chaz went back to smiling, only this time it was full of resentment and fierceness. He'd been in the life a lot longer than me and everyone liked him. I liked him too. He didn't hide much. He came at the world head-on.

Chaz reached for a zeppole, chewed it down in two bites, and then licked the sugar off his fingers. He knew how to work a crowd and get people on his side. He'd be a good boss when the time came.

He took out a cigar and clipped off the end, lit it, and took a nice long puff. He'd gotten himself under control. His voice was much quieter now, but just as filled with fury. "So you think because you're the a-number-one hitter nobody can move against you? You think we're that frightened of you? You're just another mook on the payroll. When you go down there'll be a dozen to replace you. Every man in this room has done what you do."

He looked at the firepower all around and grinned. If everyone came after me right now there'd be no way for me to fight it out. He knew it and I knew it and everyone else knew it, but that didn't mean it would ever happen. I wasn't worried. We were all one family. We'd fought off waves of attacks by outsiders.

But when you got down to it, when you got to the heart of the matter, we were all a bunch of thieves and murderers, and we didn't trust each other at all.

Most men, even wiseguys, don't like violence. They had to ramp themselves up for it. They had to throw back a few shots of liquid courage, or find a partner to go shoulder to shoulder with. They had to sneak up on the other guy and take him from behind. They had to shoot out a window during a drive-by, let the crazy noise and the action get into their blood. They had to let the rage and terror take them to the place where they lashed out in fury.

I didn't need to do any of that. That's what set me apart from the other men who killed.

Chaz glared at me, and his two soldiers tried to act rough and imposing by letting their heavily muscled bodies and sheer bulk do their talking for them. They were used to being intimidating. They had faces like rock formations. They could

crush an enemy's bones to powder if they made the effort. Their vanity and con-
fidence was scrawled in their features. They scowled at me.

I wasn't carrying. I usually didn't. In fact, I hated guns. When I did my business
I usually used a knife or my hands. I had strong, fast hands that could break stone.

Chaz was barely keeping control over himself. His best friend's death had rattled
him and I'd embarrassed him in front of the family. I hadn't handled the situation
well and there was no stopping the runaway train now. Chaz made no signal but
his boys moved out to brace me. Portman said nothing to stop them. Neither did
anyone else.

The thugs were used to men who backed away and ran. They moved in on me
with a slow and methodical pace. Instead of waiting for them to reach me, I
lunged.

It wasn't going to take much to take them. I chopped one in the throat and he
doubled over and threw up on himself. I brought my knee up into his nose and
the cartilage mashed and blood arced in an explosive fountain.

The other threw a lumbering roundhouse. I wheeled, turned my back to him,
and watched his fist come rushing over my shoulder. Facing away from him, I
caught his wrist in my right hand and pulled down hard, levering the bone over
my shoulder blade. His arm bent the wrong way across the hard muscled ridge
of my collarbone. I kept yanking on it as he screamed, his shriek eventually hitting
a high and keening note until the bone snapped. I spun and drew his body across
my hip and hurled him against the far wall.

I watched the subtle hint of fear and grudging respect swirl into Chaz's eyes. It
wasn't enough to stop him from moving against me, but he'd keep in line for at
least another few days. The rest of his crew gathered up his two wounded soldiers.

The other troops remained silent. No one pulled their piece on me. No one
else tried to muscle me. No one else bitched or grumbled. Chaz looked cool and
a touch humbled. I knew I should say something to the men, but I had no idea
what. I was hoping Portman would come in and quiet them all and bring them
around, but he just stared at me a little nervously.

"Rally your troops," I said to the capos. "Keep them in line. Wait for orders.
Chaz will take his turn soon. Until then, keep the course and watch your backs.
You know that the other mobs like to move in during these times of stress when
a don dies. And there's still someone out there who might be coming for us."

"Out there?" Chaz said. "Or is he right here with us?"

"Either way, we'll find him."

I let the dig pass. Nobody believed I would have capped the Ganooch anyway.
They knew I was loyal. They just didn't like this turn of events. It didn't matter.
Some of them wouldn't like Chaz taking over immediately either. Some of them

wanted to run the show themselves. It would all come out in the following six months or so, and then we'd all settle back into our usual routine.

The crews filed out of the warehouse. I looked out the window and watched them pulling faces and gesturing and bitching me out as they crossed the parking lot. The sky was completely clear.

Portman sat and poured himself a glass of wine.

"That was foolish," he said.

"It's only until we figure out who iced the Ganooch," I told him.

"I know that. But you should've explained it to them. You should've elaborated upon your position."

"Elaboration isn't my strong suit, Cole."

"Neither is keeping the crews in line. Instead of bringing us together in this time of trial you've got them all foaming at the mouth."

"They weren't going to listen to me no matter what I said. Chaz is too head-strong. He would've felt disrespected either way. This way, it's all in the open. They know I'm not going behind anybody's back. It'll keep them steady."

"There's going to be repercussions."

"There always is."

He poured me some wine and pushed a glass over to me. I took it and finished it in one sip. He stared up at me and shook his head again. "You're doing this so that you stand out in the spotlight. You want to see if whoever clipped the don will come after you now."

"I'm protecting *la famiglia*. I made a promise."

"We're no closer to finding out who killed Frankie."

That wasn't true. I'd had visions, seen images. Light breaking upon the darkness. Blood splashing on a tree. A beautiful blonde without a face, who wasn't a woman. Pythoness. Fishwives. Familiar spirit. I remembered what the words meant in the Bible.

"We're a little closer," I told him. "The Ganooch was murdered by witches."

That night I slipped into Gina's room and held her while she sobbed. Grandma was upstairs with the cousins and uncles and the rest of the family, half of them having flown in from Sicily. Every so often we could hear her bolt across the room and grab something off the wall, maybe Frankie's portrait, and bang it around.

"It doesn't feel like we'll ever get over this," Gina whispered.

"You will. It'll just take time."

"You're still not over your father's murder."

It was the truth. "You learn to live with it. You have no choice."

"Is that why you do what you do? Is that your way of living with it?"

"Maybe. In some fashion."

She fell back against the pillows and turned herself to me and hooked one hand around the back of my neck and drew me to her, into a kiss abandoned to pain and despair. Those emotions drove me much more deeply than love. I was comfortable among them and lifted her into my arms like a child and hugged and rocked her while she wept.

At midnight Gina fell into a restless sleep where she occasionally whimpered and whined. I stared at the ceiling and wondered how I was supposed to defend the family against someone who could kill a man just by willing it.

I nodded off at four a.m. but was awake again twenty minutes later. I turned and Gina was staring at me. Moonlight backlit her so that her face was heavy with twining shadows. She kissed me but it was almost chaste.

"It's wrong," she said.

"What is? Us being together? We're not wrong."

"How can you be so certain?"

"Why should it be wrong?"

I couldn't read her eyes in the darkness. What had attracted me to her the most was the fact that she could always keep me guessing. Others were easy to read. Once you knew what they coveted, you knew what drove them, and you could figure out exactly how far they would go to get it. I knew what went through people's minds and could take advantage of that. I could see if they were going to jump left or right, pull a gun or call the cops or make a run for it. I could predict their actions and ascertain their weaknesses.

But Gina was a paragon of cool, calm, and seeming indifference most of the time. Like her brother, she was attending Brown, attending some kind of nonsense accounting and management courses. Unlike Tommy, she was destined to be in the business. The Ganooch never wanted it for her, and Gina never said anything about it, but I could see her running the show in a couple of years when guys like Chaz Argento went up on RICO charges and the other old wiseguys retired to Miami. I always expected to do for her exactly what I did for her father and grandfather.

I was hired help. Mafia princesses didn't fool around with hired help. Well, they did, but they weren't supposed to. They were being prepped to be the wives of politicians or movie producers or Mafia princes, so they could beget other little heirs to the throne. Chaz was too old for her but I knew he'd always wanted to make a move on her. With Frankie dead, maybe he would go for it now, once he got me out of the way.

"Are you going to catch whoever killed my father?" she asked.

"Yes," I said.

"And make them pay."

"In the worst way."

"When that day comes will you let me know? I want to see it. I want to watch."

I nodded in the dark, with her head pressed against my chest. "I'll let you know. I'll let you watch."

Cole Portman knew about my mother. He knew about my fevers. He was the consigliere to the Ganucci family but could trace his family roots back to the Mayflower and was as WASPish as you could get. He didn't share our Catholic penchant for drama, history, and superstition. He didn't believe my mother had been blessed or cursed. He thought she was a schizophrenic and that I shared some of the same traits. He didn't mind so long as I remained effective. Now he was having doubts. He told me as much that morning. I had to keep an eye on him, like I had to keep an eye on everyone else.

I hit the streets. Most of the guttersnipes, low-level dealers, heisters, and wharf rats knew my name but didn't know my face. I threatened, coerced, blackmailed, and paid informants looking for any clue as to who might be behind this.

There was a Haitian mob that had risen to some power in northern Jersey and I kept wondering if some voodoo priest was sitting in front of a shrine with a shriveled doll that looked like Frankie. I kept prodding. I didn't expect much information and I didn't find any. I just wanted my enemy to know that I was out there on the prowl. I needed word to get back.

I shook things up for three days. In that time I paid out twenty grand, broke two men's arms, and clipped one overzealous bartender who snatched up a sawed-off ten-gauge hidden beneath the beer tap. No one knew anything about the hand behind the Ganooch's demise. A few mooks had heard whispers about how Chaz was planning to ice me. I wasn't surprised or worried.

The next morning, Portman phoned me to come to his home.

He lived in his own cottage on the Ganucci estate, about a quarter mile from the main house. He'd never invited me there before, but I knew every inch of it. I'd crept the place and gone through his desk, his files, every hidden cache and cubbyhole. I knew the combination to his safe. I knew the password on his password-protected computer. I knew his habits, his sexual proclivities, his preference for track lighting, the fact that he hadn't talked with his sister for thirty-seven years and the reason why.

He met me at the door, smiling sadly, his face full of near-hysteria. I could smell the scotch on his breath. He'd managed to wrap a robe around himself, but he was still wearing his PJs and slippers.

He didn't look sick. Not the way that the Ganooch had when the illness had hit him. Withered, with that deep weakness and flood of age and infirmity taking him over. Portman just appeared to be scared as hell, and he was trembling so bad that his back teeth were clicking.

"What is it?" I asked.

He ushered me inside his home, and I stepped into his small foyer. He led me to his living room, where a half-bottle of scotch stood open on a table. He hadn't been using a glass but drinking straight from the bottle.

"I noticed something when I woke this morning," he said.

"What?"

The smile played in his face, twisting his lips like softened solder. "Don't you see?"

Sunlight streamed in from the open window, the breeze carrying with it the smell of the ocean, mixing with the stink of the liquor and his morning breath.

And then I saw.

"Christ," I said.

"Goddamn right!"

I learned forward and double-checked. It was true.

Cole Portman had no shadow.

"I can feel it," he told me.

"You can feel it?"

"Writhing. It's in a bottle and someone's holding it. I can feel his hand on it. I can feel him watching it." His breathing came in ragged gasps now, the terror flooding his eyes. "It's ... it's crying. It's not just a shadow." He let out a small, crazed laugh. "I think it might be my soul."

I remembered an image that had been passed to me by my mother's seizure. A strange black bug in a jar.

I took him by the shoulders and gave him a tremendous shake, hoping it might snap him back into himself. It did nothing but rattle him a little more loose. "You can fight," I told him. "You can hold on, Cole."

"Ah God, it's an easy thing to say, but ... it's like ... it's like having ... I feel...." He couldn't put it into words. "I'm not here. I'm not all the way here. I'm missing. I've vanished. I want you to kill me. You have to end this."

"Cole—"

"You don't understand ... you·don't know what this is like. What it feels like. What it means. I'm ... I'm...."

I thought I understood enough. He wasn't in pain. He might not even be dying. But the full horror of having no soul was slowly inflicting a terrible and bewildering knowledge on him. It was something that no man should be aware of. I

was slowly watching him lose himself, his past, his mind. His eyes were completely unfocused, staring into the cosmic abyss. He smiled insanely at me and
couldn't even find his voice anymore. A newborn's gurgle escaped him. Then a
kind of mad giggle that was trapped inside his chest the way his soul was trapped
in someone's bottle.

I rose, got my arms around his throat, and snapped his neck. It took twenty
seconds, and all the while I had to listen to that laughter.

For the first time since I was fifteen, I felt my flesh crawling as fear clamped
around my heart.

I knew how to cover up a crime scene. The cops weren't going to be called in
but I had to make things look right for the rest of the troops. I set the scene to look
as if Portman had gotten drunk in his despair over Frankie's death, tried to sober
up in the shower, and taken a tumble across the bathroom floor. It would play. I
left him and headed back to the house.

It was the day of Frankie's funeral. There were mourners all over the estate. The
Sicilians were hugging each other, screaming blood oaths, and promising vengeance.

No one would miss Portman for the next few hours, everyone already had too
much on their minds. I got dressed and listened to the wails all across the house.
Grandma Ganucci was never going to settle down. She'd live another twenty years
and never wear anything but black. I fully expected her to leap down into the
grave when they lowered the coffin in.

Gina came to my room, looking beautiful and bruised, her eyes with a little
more steel in them than usual. She said, "Will you escort me?"

"Of course."

"I don't want to ride in the Caddy. Will you take your own car?"

"Sure."

"What can I do to help my mother?"

"There's nothing you can do. She'll pull it together."

"She's got to."

Tommy found us there, my hands on her shoulders in a half-embrace. He
probably already suspected Gina and I were sleeping together. He was a handsome kid wearing an uneasy smile and one of his father's best suits. The hand-
kerchief in his pocket was crumpled and dark with tears. I could guess he'd used
it to wipe his mother's face.

It would take him another decade or two before he was mature enough to realize what losing his father actually meant. He didn't know it was going to color
all of his days from this point on. He didn't know that there was a heaviness grow-

ing inside him even now that he'd have to carry for the rest of his life. He was just a kid trying to keep the women in his family from completely breaking down.

"It's time," he said.

Gina and I followed the stretch limos and drove over to St. Mark's. The church was filled to capacity and mourners were lined up out onto the street, several square blocks' worth. The feds were taking photos and video of everybody. Inside I spotted wiseguys from the Chi mob, the west coast syndicate, the Dixie mafia, the Ozark gangs, the bamboo triangle. Frankie's business associations were far-reaching.

It seemed like the entire neighborhood was there as well. You could barely hear a thing over all the weeping. Father Mike presided over mass and catalogued all of Frankie's many good deeds. All the money he'd donated to the hospital wing, the schools, the university library, the homeless shelter, the drug rehab clinic, the mother church. All of it was true, but of course it wasn't the entire truth. It wasn't any man's entire truth. Tears ran down Father Mike's face too. Gina took my left wrist and dug her nails in, determined not to fall apart in front of just about everybody she knew in the whole world.

After the service we all filed out and headed over to the cemetery. I was wrong about Grandma Ganucci. She didn't take a header into the open grave. It was Frankie's wife, Helen, who decided to give it a go. I saw her gearing up for it, her body still twitching with grief, as she took a flying run and launched herself forward.

If I hadn't been ready for someone to give it a try I wouldn't have been ready to catch her. She would have flung herself six feet down onto the coffin and broken her spine. I caught her in mid-flight and carried her back to her seat, where she almost fell over sobbing. Tommy went to his knees and wrapped his arms around her waist and buried the side of his face in her lap. After a moment, Gina did the same. I made sure that someone else besides me found Portman. One of the troops went out to see why he hadn't come to the funeral and found his body. After meeting the capos we all came to the decision that we had too many eyes focused on us and Portman should simply disappear. I put three guys on it and told them what to do and where to do it. They weren't happy and came back a few hours later smelling of lime and manure. I wondered if Portman's soul would continue thrashing in a witch's bottle for years to come or if it too would eventually just drift off and die.

In the middle of the night I awoke on fire.

I burned so badly that I rolled off the bed and onto the floor, trying to pat out flames that weren't there. I could feel smoke and steam rising off my body even if I couldn't see it. Worse, it felt like I had swallowed burning coals and I was cooking from the inside out.

The witch had finally made an attack on me.

I tried getting to the shower and seeing if I could put the fire out, but as I crawled across the floor in agony I saw a pair of beautiful legs standing before me, waiting. A foot lifted and was brought to my mouth, determined that I kiss it. When I didn't, I got a kick to the face and fell over onto my back swallowing my screams.

I looked up and she stood over me, a goddess come to demand worship and sacrifice.

She was the iconic beautiful blonde of my every man's life. She was Marilyn, and Betty Grable, Mamie Van Doren, and Jayne Mansfield. I'd always had a preference for Jayne, and as I watched, her features and form seemed to subtly shift before my eyes, until she was entirely Jayne Mansfield. My first heartfelt love.

My old man used to have a poster of Jayne on the garage wall, behind his heavy bag so he could watch her while he worked his hooks and jabs. She had been a part of my first vivid sexual fantasies, and even now I could feel the attack on my libido. She exuded carnality. She knew what would set me on fire, the way to smile, pose, turn her chin, sip air between her pouty lips.

In the real world I'd always gone for the slim, brunette, dark Mediterranean types, but this wasn't the world. This was fantasy, and in fantasy Jayne had everything I wanted. My belly twitched as my stomach acids boiled. So did my heart.

It was only partly about lust. The flesh is weak. It burns. It needs. It cries in the night. It thrashes.

But if you're stone as I am stone then it can be controlled. Pain can be compartmentalized. Desire can be stashed in the deepest black places within.

A growl escaped my throat. I was the Ganooch's number-one torpedo. I was cool. I was ice. I did what other men could not bring themselves to do. I didn't break. I didn't bend. I didn't rattle. I didn't beg.

But everything that made me who I was seemed to diminish in her presence. It was a dirty trick. This was human chemistry. It was what made me a man, the need beyond control, the draw of that inexplicable compulsion, that magic. It was sex symbol insanity. It was movie star madness.

She reached for me and I thought, No, I can resist.

I will not break. I am rock.

I thought of my capacity to inflict and endure pain. I'd suffered fever dreams for years, and this was only a little different. A will at work. Every minute that I managed to abide and bear the witchcraft, I was proving that I was stronger than they were. Whoever was concentrating on me would begin to feel fear and eventually despair because I would not succumb. No one had more willpower than I did.

The goddess fell on top of me giggling.

It was a human sound, a luscious full-bodied womanly laugh that made me want to roll with her and ignite the sheets. She reached for me and held my face in both hands. Her eyes were dark but alive with passion. They were Jayne's eyes as well as the eyes of my first love, Carmella Andagio, who drew me to her in the back of my father's Chevelle while the world kept spinning out of control around us and we burned on the seat covers only for each other. Another nasty game, another gimmick.

"I'm yours," she said. "I exist for you and you alone. Take me."

I wondered who was speaking. The witch or the demon? Or the devil himself? Should I remain silent or let it know that I wasn't going to die as easily as the Ganooch and Portman? I'd made my own blood sacrifices in the past. The mud around Sheepshead Bay was thick with my kills.

"No."

"You're on fire for me."

I knew it was the truth. I was in agony. Cramps seized me and my guts were boiling. My heart hammered and tripped along. My blood pressure had to be near stroke levels.

"You ... can't ... hurt ... me," I gasped.

Jayne wooed me, the way she wooed male moviegoers everywhere. "I don't want to hurt you. *I love you.*"

She bent over me, her perfectly draped blonde hair framing a face so beautiful that I wanted to sell whatever was left of my soul to have her for just a night, an hour, a moment.

As she dipped even closer the shadows covered her over until I couldn't even see the heavenly glint in her eyes anymore.

"*I need you. I want you.*"

I turned away and crossed my arms over my face while her body pressed against mine and she crooned in my ear. All my love and hate roared up through my brain. My hands, my strong and powerful hands, flashed out for an instant in an effort to shove her away.

She lifted me and danced with me, over me, under me, around me, and laughed the entire time.

When dawn broke, she vanished with the darkness but didn't take any of the pain away.

I laid in bed, sick for the next two hours, until Tommy came to my door to check on me. I put on my game face and pretended I was fine, took a quick shower and made my rounds across the house the way I did every morning.

The troops fell in line but they could all tell I wasn't as sharp as usual. Every time I passed a mirrored surface I saw the agony alive just beneath my drawn features and ashen skin. My belly was broiling like the fiery sword of St. Michael had skewered me.

I had a late lunch with Gina. She asked if I'd go visit her father's grave with her and I said yes. I drove her out to the cemetery and when I bent to pray I grunted in pain and almost let out a yowl.

"What's wrong?" she asked.

I said, "Heartburn."

On the way back home we hit a red light and I turned and stared at the side of her lovely face and thought she would make a wonderful wife and mother someday. Whether she took over the family business or fled from it, she would be more like Frankie than she'd probably ever know. She'd be able to do things that would stagger another person, and she'd still have the love of the neighborhood and the church and her children.

I dropped her off at the estate, parked, and walked over to the convent. Before I'd taken two steps through the front door, Sister Maeve was on the phone. I waited for the inevitable. A minute later I heard Mother Superior's footsteps ricocheting all around the place like wild gunshots.

She rounded the corner and the look on her face actually made me wince. She said, "Your visit the other day disturbed Sister Abigail greatly. She hasn't been very lucid since."

I knew that if I was burning then so was my mother.

I said, "My mother was greatly disturbed long before the other day."

"You always did have a mouth on you."

"I need to see her again."

"Absolutely not. The fevers are back. She's worse now than she has been in years."

I didn't like the idea of bulling my way into a convent and running roughshod over a bunch of nuns, but that didn't mean I wouldn't do it.

"People are dying," I said.

"People are always dying around you."

"True enough. But this is different. This is—" I hunted for a way to finish my sentence without sounding deranged or foolish.

"You're not groping for the word *evil* surely?" Mother Superior said.

"I was going to say *supernatural* or *occult*."

She actually scoffed. She squared her shoulders. She was a powerful lady. I remembered the damage she could do with a yardstick. She held her chin up proudly. Most priests and nuns I'd met had chosen the cloistered life out of tradition and cultural legacy rather than any true spiritual calling. They were as down to earth as anyone else. Mother Superior more than most. She taught Physics. She was, at heart, as much a scientist as anything else.

But she also knew, in her heart, that the otherworldly truly did exist. She'd seen it. She'd been visited by it. She'd lived with it as it existed inside of my own mother. Sister Abigail scared the hell out of everybody.

I left her there and took the stairs two at a time until I hit the fourth-floor landing. This time, the two young nuns were seated on either side of my mother's door. They looked harried and frightened. I knew it was going to be bad then.

"*La Strega*," my mother said, her habit drenched with sweat, her gaze a million miles off.

More talk of witches.

"Who is it? Who's doing this to us?"

"*Your father always did like blondes. Your grandfather too. It's in your blood. You can't help yourself. She's going to drink you alive.*"

"Ma, try to hold on. Try to help me."

She took my hand and pressed it over her lips. She kissed my hand. She cried across my knuckles. I tried to be stone but the pain made me spasm and squirm. I almost dropped to the floor. I held on and she held me. She folded my fingers so that I was cupping her tears. She touched me on the wrist and whispered, "*Infection.*"

Then she passed out.

I did too, for maybe a minute. I awoke trembling and cold. My mother's brow was unfurrowed and she seemed almost content for the moment. I carried her to her bed again. I glanced around in a fog. I stared at the saints and martyrs and knew that God himself had His eyes on me. I hadn't done a full rosary since I was thirteen. I did one now, reciting the Hail Mary over and over, and then emphasizing the Lord's Prayer every tenth prayer.

The answer was here, right in front of me, but I was too stupid to see it. I wasn't going to figure anything out. I wasn't going to be able to survive the demon indefinitely. This wasn't going to end well. Because of my lack of insight I wasn't going to be able to keep my promise and protect *la famiglia*.

Again, the maddening love of my deepest desire came to me in the night, blonde and sensual, voluptuous and glamorous, and with it arrived the heat from a billion viewings of her movies, all the male leering and ogling of her posters and centerfolds. I was the vessel for all the haunted, lonely men from around the world through the last six decades. My father's fantasies of Jayne were as much a part of me now as they ever were of him. I was a red-blooded American male who yearned for perfection, and my goddess brought it to me in the wolf's hour of the bleakest night.

"I'm yours," she said.

I burned and rolled out of bed and onto the throw rug and hid myself up against the floorboards, her flesh on me no different than licking flames. Smoke choked my lungs. I opened my mouth to speak and steam escaped.

I groaned. I snarled. I gnashed my teeth as the goddess set upon me. She tore at me like a ravenous animal, a voracious lover, her fangs and claws as ancient as the stone dagger that Abraham raised above Isaac's throat. The goddess fell on top of me, tittering and snorting like a beast.

"I'm yours," she repeated. "I exist for you and you alone. Take me. You're on fire for me. *I love you.*"

A part of me almost wanted to believe it.

I turned my face away and nearly wept.

Right after dawn, as my flesh began to cool, Gina visited my room, undid her robe and slid into bed with me. I hadn't slept a second and felt like I never would again. My brain was still boiling. My flesh stung as if ten thousand wasps had set on me. The jostling of the mattress made me stifle a moan. I let out an angry growl.

"What's wrong?" she asked.

"Nothing," I said.

She brought her lips to my back and jerked away as if in pain. She laid her hand flat between my shoulders and said, "You're burning up. Are you sick?"

"I think I caught the bug."

She didn't know what to do next. She didn't want to catch a virus but didn't want to be left alone. It was wrong of me to play against her feelings, what little she actually had for me, but it was pointless to try to make love to her after being visited by the goddess.

"Maybe you should go back to your room," I told her. "I don't want you to catch what I have."

"I need to be held," she said. "Will you do that for me?"

"Sure."

"Are you any closer to finding who murdered my father?"

"I already told you that I'd let you know and let you watch."

I wrapped my arms around her and agony roared through my chest. My hands were so weak I couldn't even give her a valid hug. My muscles were nearly useless. We spooned and I pressed my lips to the back of her neck and tried to feel the old lust and want that I used to have for her. But there was nothing there. She gripped my hands and forced me to tighten my embrace. She sighed. After a while she let out a bitter little laugh and fell asleep.

Two days later I took the subway into Manhattan and made my way through the West Village. There was an actual magic store bookended between a computer shop and an Iranian restaurant. It didn't sell magic tricks like disappearing ink or top hats with bunnies, but instead was a place where you could actually find items for rituals of witchcraft. It was called The Weird Sisters.

I hadn't finished high school or attended college but I still got the reference. The three witches in *Macbeth* were called the Weird Sisters. It might be my best shot at getting some answers or making sense out of my mother's warnings.

I stepped into the shop and a faint stink assailed me. I knew it well. It was the unmistakable smell of decomposition.

The store was packed with shelves stuffed with jars, bottles, and other containers filled with the likes of foxfire, salamander glands, dried mistletoe, salt, incense, goofer dust (graveyard), goofer dust (crematorium), dried doves' blood, owl liver, bats' wings, rooster hearts, red peppers. I wondered if they threw it around or made stew with it.

There were ceremonial daggers, chalices, and candles of every color on display. I looked for eye of newt but didn't see it anywhere. I wondered if any of this was real. I thought if it was then animal activists would be down here protesting the place night and day. I wondered if I was just on another wrong trail. I thought about my enemy out there holding a glass jar with a hopping black bug that was Cole Portman's immortal soul.

Other shelves contained reference materials, maps of haunted towns, houses, and castles. I picked up a book called *Witches and Witchcraft* and paged through it. Leaning against a case full of different-colored chalks that aided you in drawing pentagrams and circles of protection, I read about scrying mirrors, divination, the power of names, drawing down the moon, numerology, the Sabbat, how a person's true name has power over him, and how witches sometimes danced around a lightning-struck dead coven tree.

Again I thought of an image that had filled my mind the day of my mother's attack. A tree with blood splashing on it.

I kept reading and came across an article on succubi, demons in female shape that prey on men, raised by powerful sorcery.

A young woman of maybe twenty-five, who looked more girl next door than anyone who worked in a shop that sold rooster hearts and crematorium dust, appeared. She said, "I'm sorry if I kept you waiting. I didn't hear you come in. I was in the back room. Can I help you?"

I wondered what happened in the back room. I put the book back and said, "I have no idea. It depends, I suppose. Are you a good witch or a bad witch?"

It made her smile. It was a pretty smile that reached her eyes. "You've never been in a store like ours before."

"No."

"How did you find us?"

I had worked my way through most of the street informants and then started aiming myself at the Haitian influx that had suddenly populated the fringes of Bed-Stuy. I asked about voodoo dolls and zombies, and most of the dealers and thieves looked at me like I was insane. But one didn't. One started babbling and praying to Baron Samedi. He told me of shacks in Port-Au-Prince where you could buy potions to kill from afar or make someone love you. It struck a chord. We were in the greatest city on the face of the earth. Surely someone sold such things in Manhattan.

I ignored her question, glanced around, and thought of New York real estate. I imagined just how much of this stuff the owner had to push every day just to make the rent. How many hundreds or even thousands of urbanites were sitting around right now drawing circles of protection around themselves in fifth-floor walk-ups.

"My name's Kendra," she said.

"Names have power."

"Yes, they do."

She had green eyes flecked with gold, blonde hair fixed into a bouncing pony tail. She was a cheerleader type. I could imagine her on the sidelines doing kicks and clapping as the QB sprinted toward the end zone. But her clothing wrecked the girl-next-door image. She wore a wrap covered with the Weird Sisters logo, three witches with their backs to a boiling cauldron. One a crone, one a kind of buxomly mother figure, and the last a seductive teen. On her blouse were ancient symbols, inscriptions in Latin, and verses from the Bible. Her leggings were black with bright white star constellations and signs of the zodiac.

"How about making a man age fifty years almost overnight?" I asked. "Which one of these books will show me how to do that?"

It made Kendra's face close up like a fist. "No one's ever asked before."

"What about stealing a soul? Where can I learn how to poach a man's shadow, his soul, and stick it in a jar and watch it writhe in torment?"

She set her lips and her expression shifted to sadness, interest, and futility. "I can't help you with anything like that. The things we sell are mostly for wiccan rites, pagan beliefs that are in keeping with the harmony of the earth."

The frustration and anger had welled in me. I hadn't slept in days. I was weak and my resolve was waning. "Who can send the world's most perfect woman to love a man to death? Does that take some salamander glands or doves' blood?"

She glanced around but we were alone in the store. She stepped in closer to me, her eyes growing more serious. The dimples faded. Her chin came up.

"Something's happened to you," she said.

"Yes."

She looked deep into my face and saw something there that put a real fear into her. "You were talking about yourself. You're the one who's afflicted."

I nodded.

"You admit it easily. A lot of people can't. Their rationale refuses to accept such possibilities. They think they're imagining things or going crazy. But you, you believe."

"Yes."

"You've had some past experience with the occult."

I didn't know what to say to that so I didn't say anything. I nodded again.

"The world's most perfect woman loving a man to death isn't a woman at all," Kendra said. "You must realize that. It's a succubus. A demonic entity that drains the life from its intended victim. I can see the stress and strain in your features. You've been trying to fight it, haven't you?" Before I could answer she continued. "Good. You're strong, very strong. You still have a little time left."

"What's the best way I can use that time?" I asked. "How do I find whoever is doing this to me?" I ran my hands over the spines of the books. "Do you know of anyone who is capable of this kind of thing?"

I sounded almost whiny. The sickness was throwing me off balance. I knew better than most people that anyone was capable of almost anything. Looking at me, could this girl guess what I did for a living?

"The question is, do *you* know anyone with that capacity?" Kendra said. "Who hates you that much?"

"It's a long list."

"It's a short one, a very short one. You have to understand that there's a balance," she explained. "Where there's grace, there's depravity. Where there's salvation, there's Satan. Most of the practitioners will use these rituals and elements for peaceful and serene reasons. But some will use them for evil means. There's no way to tell who will do what. Whatever is in their hearts will lead them to taking positive energy and bending it toward ill. The tools aren't bad in and of themselves, but a corrupt intention will use them to an immoral end."

"Have you met anyone here like that? Anyone who could do the things I mentioned?"

"Everyone has the capacity. You don't have to raise a demon. All you have to do is hate enough and focus enough and a demon will find you. The devil always knows your heart."

Now that felt very true to me.

"So what can I do?" I asked.

"There are prayers and spells of protection."

"Care to whip up a few?"

She rubbed the back of her hand against her nose. It was a cute nose. She sort of smiled again, trying to remain amiable despite the heaviness of our discussion. I wondered what had diverted her into working in a shop like this when she should be at some booth on Coney Island letting the boys ogle and flirt with her and buy her cotton candy. Because of my own lost childhood I had romanticized notions of the world where pretty girls like this were concerned. I hoped I hadn't brought a curse to her front step.

She said, "Maybe I can help."

"I can pay you."

"Don't taint my efforts. Let my willingness be pure."

"Okay."

She turned and moved up the aisle toward the back of the store, her ponytail swaying. I thought if I had grown up next door to her or someone like her my life would have taken a very different course. But that was probably nothing more than wishful thinking.

I took another book off the shelf and continued reading, learning about how pagan rites could be either white—right-handed, clockwise, righteous, and graceful—or black—left-handed, widdershins or counter-clockwise, flying in the face of the natural order of the world.

The electronic bell signaled that someone had stepped into the store.

I'd made another mistake and left myself out in the open, too close to the front entrance. In the center of the aisle there was nowhere for me to run as Chaz Argento walked up with two soldiers who already had their weapons drawn. I'd never seen either of them before, which told me Chaz had farmed out for hard hitters loyal only to him and not to the Ganucci family. He was making his play.

I shut the book, put it back on the shelf, and our eyes met. Chaz let out a slow humorless smile.

He gestured for one of his legbreakers to search the store. The muscle-bound, no-neck thug stalked off and I thought I had to move now, while they were split up. I wasn't packing a gun but I had my knife. As a rule you didn't throw blades, but I was good enough that I could hit the remaining soldier's barrel chest. The knife wouldn't kill him, but it would hurt and scare him, and the blood would spook Chaz. I might just have enough of a diversion so that I could wade in and do some real damage.

Except it didn't happen. Kendra had already been on her way back to me and was only a few feet up the next aisle. The thug returned with her three seconds later, one huge hand clamping her shoulder.

The pain made her body twist before him, and she couldn't so much as get out a groan. He shoved the girl at me and she tumbled and hit the floor at my feet.

"Don't be a moron, Chaz," I said.

"Stop talking that way to me! I'm the new skipper. The Ganooch is gone. His consigliere is dead. Someone's got to run the business and I'm in line. You have no say. You have no right."

"I'm only asking for you to give me a few more days."

It got him laughing. "What kind of a mook do you make me for? You think you can bounce my crew off the walls and talk down to me and there'll be no repercussions? You think that's how things happen in this world?"

"We can work together."

"You're not listening to me. You never listen to anybody, now do you?"

Maybe it was true. I didn't go out drinking with the boys, didn't bust chops, didn't play high-stakes poker in the back rooms. Maybe I'd kept myself a little too far out of things for anyone in the crew to trust me now.

Chaz's boys each held a 9mm on me.

Kendra whimpered, "Please, I didn't do anything."

"Sorry, miss," Chaz said, sounding genuinely apologetic. "Maybe if you'd been a good little girl and gone to church instead of dealing with all this heathen crap you wouldn't be in such a tight spot right now."

Chaz was trying to ramp himself up for the hit. He was building drama, making himself angry, indulging himself and basking in the dreamy glow of how good life would be once I was out of the way.

Kendra did what any normal person would do. She made a break for it. Her fight-or-flight response took over and her terror forced her to run down the aisle away from me. I almost reached out for her. One of the goons snapped off a shot. It was low and took Kendra in the small of her back.

She crumbled and turned over twice, the ponytail still wagging, her expression falling in on itself as the dreaded understanding of her own impending death overtook her. No handsome boy would ever take her out dancing again. Her face filled with an immense loss and her gaze settled on me. She didn't hate me even now; she was just astonished by how events had unfolded like this, so quickly, so badly, in an unstoppable chain of fated moments. She tried crawling but only made it a couple of feet before she lay dead with a kidney shaped pool of blood spreading toward the shelves of her indifferent and useless magical books. It also washed toward me.

"That was a mistake," I told Chaz.

"I've made 'em before," he said, "I'll make a few more before my time is up."

"No you won't."

I reached for the goofer dust and hurled it at Chaz and his men. The instant I released the jar I spun aside and drew my knife. The glass broke against Chaz's chest, nearly knocking him down, and sent a cloud of ash up. Two shots roared past me. That was the problem with hiring freelancers, you never really knew how good they were in a tight spot. In less than a second I hurled the blade as well.

I was still weak, but there was enough force behind my throw for the blade to take one of the thugs in the neck. It barely nicked the guy's carotid but it was enough to get a high arc of arterial spray going. He overreacted and started screaming as his blood spurted up in front of his eyes. The dust had them coughing and teary-eyed. I marched in on them thinking, My hands are fast. They can break rock. I'm a torpedo. I don't waver. I don't stand down. An innocent is dead because of me. I have the willpower to beat my enemy. I can outlast them all.

I wasn't anywhere near form, but I didn't have to be. Chaz turned and tried to bolt. A moment later the other two made a run as well. It didn't matter. I took some time. I was lucky the store was empty. Hardly anybody believed in magic anymore.

On the subway ride back I started to fall asleep. I figured the succubus wouldn't attack on a train full of people, but for all I knew it never manifested in the world anyway, only in my mind. I had just killed three men and it somehow made me content. Maybe because I had lived through it, maybe because I was simply evil.

As the train slipped down the tunnel under the East River and the darkness settled in around us, I nodded off enough for another fever dream to hit. I could hear myself panting in the car. Sweat dripped down my neck and over the knot of my tie. It was too dark to see anything but I looked down anyway and saw Kendra there holding my left hand. So lovely and cute and with that smile that could have altered my entire life. She said, "*Infection.*"

I snapped fully awake with a start.

I knew where to find the witch.

Tommy came in wearing one of the Ganooch's suits and smelling of his old man's aftershave. I hadn't expected Tommy to fall for such a commonplace convention as following in his father's footsteps, but here it was.

He took a stance that also mimicked the Ganooch, shoulders high, hands clasped together low.

He said, "I'm taking over the business. I'm going to fight Chaz for the leadership."

"You won't have to," I told him. "Chaz is dead."

"He is? How? When?" He cocked his head at me. "You?"

"Yes."

"Why? For me?"

It got a chuckle up from deep down in my chest. "Tommy, you don't have the heart for this business, but if you want to give it a go, I won't try to talk you out of it. But I can tell you now that you'll be dead within three months. Nobody will follow you. Whoever claims to be loyal to you will just be setting you up. All your men will filter over to one of the other families or move on out to LA or Chi."

His handsome, youthful face looked almost bratty. "And you? Won't you be my right hand?"

"No."

"Why not?" His voice was tight. "Are you running out too?"

"In a matter of speaking, Tommy."

He squared his shoulders like he wanted to take a poke at me. I stared at him and saw a reckless boy trying to step up and be the man of a family that performed acts he would never be able to fully understand or accept.

I said, "Go back to college, Tommy. Learn some other skill."

"But what about...?"

"Don't worry about your mother or grandmother. Provisions have been made. There's enough money floating around from all the legal enterprises, stocks, bonds, money markets, and bank accounts to keep things running exactly as they are for a very long time. Nobody's going to move grandma out onto the street."

"And the crew? The captains?"

"Let it all dismantle itself. You won't have to lift a finger. It'll all play out the way it's meant to, and by the time you graduate and get a job on Wall Street you'll be head of all the above-board businesses."

He seemed to consider it seriously. He looked at me and gave a grimace and a half-nod, perhaps agreeing with me or maybe only coming to some different decision. I didn't know and didn't really care anymore.

I walked downstairs to the kitchen, unlocked the wine cellar, and went down into the depths where I found a rare bottle of Amarone. The Ganooch had paid sixteen grand for it. I didn't know why. I opened it and took a deep pull, enjoying the full-bodied taste of the fat Corvino grapes that they let turn to raisins for a stronger concentration of flavor. Or so the Ganooch told us around the dining room table one evening.

It reminded me of the wine we used to drink at mass during communion. I wanted to confess my sins but there wasn't enough time. There would never be enough time for that.

I left the half-emptied bottle on the floor and headed back up the cellar stairs. I walked the main house. The place had a near deathly quiet. I passed our soldiers, looking uncertain and clearly planning their defection. I heard Helen weeping inside her bedroom. I wanted to let her know that more pain was coming, but it wouldn't last, and if she just held on a little longer she might find a better life for her waiting down the line. I didn't think she could, though. I suspected she was going to off herself soon, and there was nothing I could do about it.

I kept prowling. Grandma recited the rosary. I pressed my forehead to her door. I listened to her reciting the Hail Mary in Italian, over and over again, maybe for the ten thousandth time in her life, maybe for the millionth. I stood there for twenty minutes, her voice sometimes growing stronger, sometimes only a whisper, the same prayer almost sounding like it was becoming other words and appeals as her tone shifted and my concentration waned. I'd thought I was special but I wasn't. She had more willpower than I did. She was a truly powerful woman able to find fortitude in her grief. She would outlive me.

I moved down the corridor. Tommy's door stood open. He had several suitcases open on his bed and he was placing his folded clothes carefully inside them. I thought if any of us had a chance, it might be him.

I came to Gina's room. I put my hand on the doorknob and could feel a kind of electrical buzz going through it. But the strange tingling didn't really touch my hand. Instead it danced through me and shocked the back of my head.

I tried the door and it was locked. I put more effort into it, braced my shoulder against the wood and exerted pressure. The door itself wasn't holding me back but some other force was. A will at work.

I gritted my teeth and kept trying. I glanced down at my wrist and spotted four small black indents in my flesh. I'd barely noticed them before but now they stood out against the thick blue veins twining up my forearm.

That's where I'd become infected.

On the day of the Ganooch's funeral. That night was the first time the succubus, the goddess, had come to me.

I remembered the moment I'd received those near-invisible indents. During the service, Gina had taken my left wrist and dug her fingernails in, determined not to fall apart in church.

Whatever venom she'd set loose in me had begun to do its job right then.

I had my own will at work. My forehead began to heat. I clenched my jaws together and gritted my teeth. I had just murdered three men. I had been the cause of an innocent woman's death. The devil was here.

The wood began to crack as I pressed my weight against it harder and harder. I wanted to keep it as quiet as possible. I heard laughter inside the room. I might've even chuckled a bit myself. Where there's grace, there's depravity.

The jamb began to buckle, the lock gave way, and I stepped in.

Gina was seated at her vanity, wearing nothing but a silken see-through shawl, brushing her hair. The tri-fold mirror situated around her didn't reflect her face from three sides. Instead, it showed different, shifting images. From the brief amount of reading I'd done in the Weird Sisters shop I knew this was a scrying mirror, magical glass used to show future or past events.

I saw the two of us in bed. My father's garage with the poster of Jayne Mansfield on the wall. Me and Frankie playing racquetball. I saw myself snapping Portman's neck. I watched my old man die. It hadn't been the Jamaicans who'd killed him like I'd long thought. I watched my mother rise from a crouch behind a cluster of trash cans and murder him with a butcher knife while he'd stumbled drunkenly toward home.

It didn't surprise or startle me. It didn't hurt me. My old man deserved what he got. I was only bothered that my mother had given her life away to the church out of guilt, when she shouldn't have felt ashamed for doing what she'd done out of self-defense. He would've beaten her to death eventually.

Gina continued drawing the brush through her gleaming black hair.

I wondered how long she'd been studying me from afar. Maybe the devil whispered all my secrets in her ear. I wanted to know when this had all started. When she'd taken the first step down the path to becoming a witch. But it didn't matter. Like Kendra said, as soon as evil was in your heart, you didn't have to go looking for the devil. The devil would find you.

"Why don't you change the channel on that thing," I said, "and watch moments from your own life?"

"I do," Gina said, almost primping even though she couldn't see her own face in the mirror. "I've witnessed all my own mistakes, all the secrets that my father tried to hide from me."

"He hid them for a reason."

"Not a good enough one." She turned in her seat, the curves of her lithe body accented by the draping of her garment. I saw the hate in her face then. It had been tamped down and hidden for a long time, but now it seeped to the surface and darkened and deepened every line. "You feel like a fool, don't you?"

"Yes. I should've started off looking closer to home for the enemy."

"That's what I had to do," she said.

"Your father wasn't your enemy. Neither was Portman. Or me."

"You all were," she said. Her voice was tight and bitter. "You just didn't fully understand it. You thought I was so accepting. So involved. I was born blood-stained thanks to this family, this business, you people."

"Everyone's born bloodstained, Gina. That's just the natural way."

Beside the perfumes, combs, and creams on the vanity sat a trembling glass bottle. Inside I could see an odd black bug crawling and leaping and fluttering about. Portman's shadow.

I took another step into the room. It hurt like hell and I almost went to my knees. It was like trying to walk through unseen razor wire. I grunted and my blood began to burn. The edges of my vision filled with colorful lights. I tried to shake my head clear. The cramps returned and nearly crippled me. The succubus didn't have to appear at night. It didn't have to appear at all. Whatever power it had, Gina had as well. It was her will. You don't have to call a demon because the demon will always find you.

"Why did you do this?" I asked. I had to breathe through my teeth. "Because you wanted the business?"

"Haven't you understood a word that I've said so far? It's because I hate this business and everyone associated with it."

"Even me?"

"You most of all."

"Then why wasn't I first on your hit list?"

"You were."

"Then why aren't I dead yet?"

'There's nothing to kill in you. There's nothing alive in you." She smiled at me then and there wasn't anything in it that was the girl I thought I knew. "That's why you could only be murdered with lust. But not love."

Maybe it was true. I tried to find something to say but there wasn't anything. I took another step toward her and the succubus tore at me. I hit the floor.

Gina stood over me and said, "I was raised in evil and that evil has stained me. I can feel all my father's victims screaming from their graves. All of the men you've killed. You think I'm lying. I know Chaz is dead. He's being flayed by a duke of Hell, who's whipping him with a cat o' nine tails made from two-thousand-year-old leather and bone. It's the same whip used to beat Christ along his walk through Jerusalem to Golgotha, the hill of skulls."

I thrashed on the floor, my clothes steaming. The succubus' claws raked my flesh. It felt like the goddess was tearing at me from the inside. I could feel her scraping at my spine, gashing my kidneys, squeezing my heart.

I'd sworn I would protect the family. I had failed in my promise. I'd held Gina in the cold night and whispered that I would keep her safe. I had been in the presence of an abiding madness and hadn't known it. And I'd made pledges to her that I would never let anything happen to her.

"Are you afraid?" she asked.

I couldn't even speak. I tried to shake my head no and could feel my eyelashes curling from the heat. My tears seemed to be boiling even before they fell. I could hear the demon's voice. It was Jayne's voice. It was Gina's voice. It was Lilith's voice, and every furious woman's voice going back to the moment the Garden of Eden had been locked behind humanity.

"*I love you.*"

Chaz was being flayed in hell, and he wasn't alone. Frankie would be there too. I'd soon join them. I'd been resolved to that for years. I was my own man. I was stone in the night, and I couldn't be broken.

Sweat slithered into my eyes. Gina bent and undid my tie and opened my collar. She drifted to her vanity again. I watched light reflecting off the sharpened edge of metal. I thought she had drawn out a ceremonial dagger, but in reality it was only a butterfly blade.

It was her father's weapon of choice when he wanted to make a point. When he thought the troops were skimming too much off the top he'd wait until one of them was reaching across the table and then he'd stab the guy in the back of the hand. Or he'd slash the mook on the forehead, right at the hairline where the blood vessels were close to the surface of the skin and any small wound would pour blood into a person's eyes. You didn't have to do much to get drama out of a butterfly knife.

When I used one I went for the short ribs and twisted the blade up into my victim's heart.

Gina did the same. She was fast and I was weak. I tried rolling away but couldn't make it. She caught me low in the left side and the knife immediately punctured

my lung. I started huffing air as she tried to angle the blade up into my heart. It
almost worked.

I was damned but I wasn't dead yet. I grabbed her around the wrist and fought
with her. The blade sawed sideways into my belly. I snapped my arm down hard
and managed to force her to let go of the knife handle. The blade remained stuck
in the side of my chest.

I forced my lips to part. I made myself say the words.

"Gina Ganucci."

Names had power.

"Angelina Ganucci."

It seemed almost silly, expecting a person's name to save me from the ledge
of death. But the words were more than sounds. They represented everything
that you were, all that you might be. Saying her name put definition on her. The
scrying mirror began to pulse with new images. I said Gina's name again. I saw
her as a little girl, enraged at her father, hiding in the dark. I watched her reading
from stupid books on magic and performing silly rites of magic that meant nothing except it showed a willingness to give yourself over to malignance. I watched
the two of us making love for the first time. Afterward, while I slept, she poured
her malice in my ear.

She reached down and tried to grip the handle of the blade with both hands,
but I drew her forward into an embrace instead. I held onto her. I thought a part
of me had managed to love her as much as I was capable of loving any woman. I
tightened my hold and kissed her throat. She struggled and beat at my chest and
snarled in my face. I kissed her again.

"Even if you kill me the spell won't stop," she said. "The demon will follow you
until you die."

"Maybe that's how it should be."

"Do you want to know why I didn't steal your soul?"

"I already know."

"*Because you don't have one.*"

"Goodbye, Gina."

My hands moved then, doing amazing and savage things almost without my
consent. When it was done I was red and wet up to the elbows and some of the
fever had left me. I climbed to my feet and pulled the knife out of my side. A gout
of blood followed. I tore up a bed sheet and tightened a makeshift bandage over
the wound. The bleeding wouldn't stop but it had slowed some.

I picked up the bottle holding Portman's shadow and smashed it. I watched a
liquid-like blackness pour free, rise, curl through the air, and vanish. Then I gripped
myself across the belly trying to keep my guts in and stumbled out the door.

I staggered through the neighborhood, leaving a spattered trail on the sidewalks. Shop owners called to me. I scuffed chalk-drawn hopscotch boards and felt bad about it. Kids followed saying, "Mister, you know you're bleeding?"

I made it to the church in time for evening mass and fell into the back pew as I listened to the benediction of the blessed sacrament. I hadn't heard it for years. It was an invocation for divine help, spiritual guidance, and forgiveness. I wondered if there was still time for a man like me to regain his soul. I listened to my blood dripping onto the floor and felt a little sorry for whoever had to clean up the mess after me.

I leaned my head back and listened to the prayers from the few parishioners. I found a strange comfort in it, something that led me back to my childhood when I was an altar boy and had a firm faith that God would reward and protect me someday.

I heard Mother Superior's footsteps in the vestibule before I saw her. I glanced up and there she was with two nuns I didn't know and my mother. They had her by the elbows and were helping to carry her along as they all came toward me. Her habit was soaked with sweat and she was holding herself about the waist. I could see she was in terrible pain. We were still sharing dreams and sorrow, visions and misery.

"Hello, Ma."

She didn't respond. Her eyes had that thousand-yard stare like she was looking through me into the abyss. Her dry, cracked lips framed sentences I couldn't distinguish. I thought, She'll be rid of me soon and be much better off without the burden. Maybe my death would give her a fresh chance at life in or out of the convent. I tried to imagine her a normal, happy woman planting roses in a garden out on Long Island, a second husband mowing the lawn, a dog romping around. I tried desperately to hold the picture in my mind, but it kept flitting away.

They helped to slide her in beside me and the nuns I didn't know tore open my shirt and started working on my wounds. A lot of nuns seemed to have some kind of emergency training. I don't know where they got it from but I'd seen them do this kind of thing before. They applied pressure and checked my pulse rate and tried to stem the flow of my blood. They failed. Then one ran off to call 911.

The Mother Superior gave me the same kind of glare that I'd be met with at the gates of heaven. God would look at me with no less disappointment and anger.

I grinned at her. "Say a prayer ... for me."

"I've said thousands for you."

"Thanks for trying."

"No one's beyond redemption."

"You almost ... said that ... with a straight face."

I laid out on the pew and listened to the benediction echoing across the high ceilings, the stained glass windows, the stone images of Christ's agony in the twelve stations of the cross. Then it came to an abrupt end as the priest finally caught wise to what was happening at the back of the church. I heard some muted shouts then and footfalls on the marble.

I rested my head in my mother's lap and she pressed her lips to my ear and began murmuring indecipherable words in a language beyond language that soon began to make a bizarre kind of sense. I managed to eke out a rough cough of laughter as the light drew away farther and farther and separated from the oncoming rush of endless darkness and black fire.

Pokky Man
A Film by Vernor Hertzwig

By

Marc Laidlaw

VERNOR HERTZWIG
FILMMAKER

In 2004 I was contacted by Digito of America to review some film footage they had acquired in litigation with the estate of a young Pokkypet Master named Hemlock Pyne. While I have occasionally played board games such as Parchesi, and various pen-and-paper role-playing games involving dwarves and wizards, in vain hopes of escaping the nightmare ordeals that infest my soul, I was hardly the target audience for the global phenomenon of Pokkypets. I knew only the bare lineaments of the young man's story—namely that he had been at one time considered the greatest captor of Pokkypets the world had ever known. Few of these rare yet paradoxically ubiquitous creatures had escaped being added to his collection. But he had turned against his fellow Trainers, who now hurled at him the sort of venom and resentment usually reserved for race traitors. The childish, even cartoonish aspects of the story were far from appealing to me, especially as spending time on a hundred or so hours of Pokkypet footage would mean delaying my then-unfunded cinematic paean to those dedicated paleoanthropologists who study human coprolites or fossil feces. But there was an element of treachery and tragedy that lured me to look more carefully at the life and last days of Hemlock Pyne, as well as the amount of money Digito was offering. I found the combination irresistible.

HEMLOCK PYNE
POKKY MASTER

To be a Pokky Captor was for me the highest calling—the highest calling! I never dreamed of wanting anything else. All through my childhood, I trained for it. It was a kind of warrior celebration ... a pokkybration, you might say, of the warrior spirit. I lived, ate, breathed, drank, even pooped the Pokky spirit. Yes, pooped. Because there is dignity in everything they do. When it comes to Pokkypets, there is no room for shame—not even in pooping. In a sense, I was no different from many, many other children who dream of being Pokky Captors. The only difference between me and you, children like you who might be watching this, is that I didn't give up on my dream. Maybe it's because I was such a loser in every other part of my life—yeah, imagine that, I know it's difficult, right?—but I managed to pull myself free of all those other bonds and throw myself completely into the world of Pokkypets. And I don't care who you are or where you are, but that is still possible today.

VERNOR HERTZWIG

Hemlock Pyne's natural enthusiasm connected him ineluctably with the childish world of Pokkypets—the world he never really escaped. The more I studied his footage, the more I saw a boy trapped inside a gawky man-child's body. It was no wonder to me that he had such difficulty relating to the demands of the adult world. In cleaving to his prejuvenile addictions, it was clear that Pyne hoped to escape his own decay, and for this reason threw himself completely into a world that seems on its face eternal and unchanging. The irony is that in pursuing a childish wonderland, he penetrated the barrier that protects our fragile grasp on sanity by keeping us from seeing too much of the void that underlines the lurid cartoons of corporate consumer culture, as they caper in a crazed dumbshow above the abyss.

PITER YALP
ACTOR

I think we knew, and assumed Hemlock knew, where was this was probably heading. And it's hard to see a person you care for, a friend of many years, make the sorts of decisions he made that put him ever deeper into danger. It didn't really help to know that it was all he cared for, that all this danger was justified in a way by passion, by love. And when you saw him light up from talking about it, it was hard to argue. He'd never had anything like that in his life. I mean, he'd been through a lot. Coming back to Pokkypets, sure it seemed childish at first, but he was so disconnected from everything anyway, we had to root for him, you know? But we still feared for him. He never did anything halfway, you know? Whenever he started anything, you always knew he was going to push it past any extreme you could imagine. So it was only sort of ... sort of a shock, but more of a dreaded confirmation, when we heard the news. I remember I was in the kitchen nuking some popcorn for dinner, and the kids were watching Pokkypets on, you know, the Pokkypets network ... and then our youngest said, "Look, it's Uncle Hemlock!" Which seemed weird at first because why would he be on their cartoon? But then I saw it was the Pokkypets Evening News, and even though the sound was turned up full, I found I couldn't hear what the anchorman was saying. I just stared at the picture of Hemlock they'd put up there ... the most famous shot of him, crouched in the Pokkymaze, letting an injured Chickapork out of a Poachyball ... and from the way the camera slowly zoomed back from the photo, I knew right then ... he wouldn't be coming back to us this time.

AUGUSTINE "GUST" MASTERS
SEAPLANE PILOT

I was friends with Hem for years and years, used to fly him out here to the Pokky-maze in midsummer, come and collect him before fall settled in; I'd check in from time to time to see how he was doing, and drop off the occasional supply. He was a special sort of guy, and there won't never be another like him. For one thing, he was fearless, as you can imagine you'd have to be to try living right here like he did. From where we're standing, you can watch the migratory routes of about 150 different types of Pokkypets; everything from the super common Pecksniffs, to the Gold-n-Silver Specials, to the uniques like Abyssoid, who comes up out of this here lake once a year for about thirty seconds at 8:37 a.m. on September 9, and only if the 9th happens to fall on a Tuesday. Really it's a Captor's dream, or would be if it wasn't a preserve. Hem came out here every year, and never once tried to capture or collect a single one of the Pokkys ... in fact they were more likely to collect him. He got adopted by Chickapork to the extent you couldn't tell who belonged to who. Anyway ... he made it a point of pride that he never carried a Poachyball, that he was here to protect the Pokkypets, to prevent them from being collected. When he was young he was a heck of a Captor, but once he put that aside, that was it. He didn't try charming them with flutes or putting them to sleep;

he didn't freeze or paralyze them with any of Professor Sequoia's Dust Infusion, or Thunderwhack a single one. He came out empty-handed, and tried to make a Pokky out of himself, I guess. If I had to pick one thing, I guess I'd say that right there was his undoing. That and Surlymon.

VERNOR HERTZWIG

What others saw as evidence of everything from low self-image to schizophrenia, was to Hemlock Pyne nothing more than a kind of dramatic stage lighting, necessary to cast an imposing shadow over a world that considered him but a small-time actor in a community theater production. It did not matter to the rest of the world that in this tawdry play, Hemlock Pyne had the leading role; but to Pyne himself, nothing else mattered. He had cast himself in the part of the renegade Captor who would give himself completely to his beloved Pets. That it was to be a tragic role, I suspect would not have stopped him. And while he seems to have had premonitions of his fate, he could have asked any number of those who spent their lives working in and around the Pokky Range, and have heard many predictions that would end up remarkably close to the eventual outcome.

AUGUSTINE "GUST" MASTERS

Right here is where I came in for my usual rendezvous, at the appointed time, ready to take him out of here. At first I thought maybe I had the day wrong, because usually I'd expect to see him with all his gear packed up and waiting here on the shore. It was later in the year than he'd ever stayed, not our usual date, so I thought it was my mistake, and I went hollering up the hillside trail here toward his camp, figuring maybe he could use a hand packing up his stuff. But halfway up the trail here I got a really funny feeling ... not a nice feeling at all. I never travel here without a few extra Poachyballs, and some Coma Flakes—I mean, I'm no Hemlock, I come prepared for anything. And I was just freeing up a Poachyball in case I had to make an emergency capture, when I heard this grumbling in the brush off to the side of the trail, and very clearly I could hear a big old Pokkypet crawling around in there, just saying its name over and over again so there was no mistaking what I was up against. Going, "Surly ... Surly ..." Like that. Just a nasty old Pokky, saying its name like a warning ... that one bad note over and over again.

Well, I don't mind saying it scared me, and forgot about trying to catch it, since that's a tough one to collect even if you're fully prepared. I didn't have any Pokkypets of my own to back me up. So I hightailed it back to the plane, and took off, just cold and sweatin', my guts full of ice water, you know. I tried to get Hemlock on his radio a couple times, but no answer there, and I was starting to believe we weren't going to get any more answers at all. I brought the plane in low over the maze, low as I could, and the way Hem would hide his tent in the trees I knew it would be hard to get a clear picture of what was going on there—but as I was flying over, the wind swept over pretty hard. Banked me a bit just as it was parting the trees around his campsite, and I got one clear look that I'll never forget. Right below me, the tent had been flattened so that the poles were sticking up out of it. Gear was scattered everywhere—clothes, camera equipment, pots and pans. And Hemlock was scattered everywhere too, in and around the tent. I hardly knew what I was seeing. His head staring up at me, on the other side of the site from his chest; an arm here, a leg there. I couldn't tell if his eyes were open, but I didn't see how they could be. I figured he had to be sleeping after an attack like that. I knew I'd need help getting him out of there, so I banked into the wind and headed back to town.

HEMLOCK PYNE
10 DAYS BEFORE THE END

This is Surlymon. He's a very old Pokkypet, and we're just getting to know each other. I'm not usually here in the Pokkymaze this late in the year, but I had a little upset at the airport and decided I was not ready to leave my Pokky friends just yet to return to all the … all the bullpoop and the hassle of … of poopy humans back in the so-called real world. Just wasn't ready. So here I am, and some of my old friends seem to have moved on, and some new Pokkys have moved in. It's the migratory time, you see … all a completely natural part of the Pokkypet cycle, and pretty exciting to see it in action. Not to say that there isn't danger here— there's plenty of it. But that's what keeps me going. Nobody else could do what I do … give themselves to the protection of the Pokkypets the way I do. And they respect me for it. They know that I have the best of intentions … that I'd be one of them if I could. But in the meantime, I'm getting to know Surlymon here … getting to earn his trust. Isn't that right, Surlymon? We're getting to know each other. Yes we are! Yes we are! Now … hey … HEY! Watch it! Back off! That is not cool, Surlymon. Not cool. Good, Pokky. Okay, good old Pokky. Yes, you're a good old boy, I know, I know. I love you. I love you. I'm sorry I had to snap at you like that. I'm Hemlock, okay? Hemlock! Hemlock! Hemlock! I love you. Hemlock loves you. Hemlock. Hemlock. … Hemlock.

AUGUSTUS "JUSTICE" PEACE
HELICOPTER PILOT

I've known Gust for years, and through him I knew Hemlock Pyne, though we weren't what you'd call close. That day he came back with news about Hemlock's troubles, I could tell he'd seen something that nobody should see. Well, we called the Pokky Park Service, which is basically every other person around here, and we got three Captors together and I took us out in the chopper. We landed on Baldymon Hill, which overlooks the Pokkymaze, and they went on down there while I kept an eye on the chopper, ready to light out at a moment's notice. I could hear them when they caught up with the Surlymon. They had some pretty tough pets with 'em, but that soncfabitch was tough. It took all three Captors in full Pokkybattle, and each one of them used at least three Poachyballs, setting their own pets on the Surlymon. It took eight—eight!—Pokkypets to wear down that Surlymon. I think the final attack was a full-on Typhon-Crash-Mastery move, and then the Surlymon finaly went into slumber. It was only then that the thing was vulnerable and they could poach it. I heard all this, mind; I didn't see any of it ... but I'll tell you, every time I heard that thing giving out its call, my blood ran cold. "Surly! Surly!" Well, I can't do it. It was a horrible sound, though. When they finally came crashing through the underbrush dragging the Poachyball, with their own poor little pets limping along behind, the Captors looked like they'd been involved in the struggle themselves ... and I don't mean psychically.

But then it was over to me and Gust. He led me back down the hill and into the maze, to the campsite, and there was Hemlock Pyne in a dozen pieces. It was weird and awful. Gust called his name a few times, trying to wake him up, because we didn't really realize the extent of it yet.... It was a sleep like nothing we'd ever seen. I had some Sudden Stir powder with me and I sprinkled it in his eyes, but it didn't do a thing. And I've never seen a Pokkypet or Captor yet who could sleep through that stuff. After a while we decided we'd best get him into town to the Pokky Clinic, so we gathered up the pieces. Filled four Poachyballs with the parts. That was all we had to carry him in.

MADRONA SEQUOIA
FRIEND, POKKYOLOGIST

What Hemlock wanted was a way to mutate into a Pokkypet himself. He was very, very uncomfortable being in his own skin, especially when it meant he was a Captor or Master of Pokkypets. He wanted to merge with the Pokkys ... become one of them, share in their alchemic process. Hemlock sensed a transformative power in them, and he wanted this for himself. When he was studying with me, we went through the triadic life cycle of the typical healthy Pokkypet, following its course in many, many creatures. When he first went out into the Pokky Range with the idea of studying and protecting the pets, you know, he placed himself in the habitat of the Pigletta. It was a good fit for him, since they are such friendly creatures, but his ulterior motive was to bond so closely with one that it would allow him to stay with it through all its transformations. Of course, everyone who adopts a Pigletta feels that theirs is special, and that they have a unique friendship ... but in Hemlock's case I think there is a real argument for this. After all, he had stopped collecting at that point; he never stunned his Pokkypet or trapped it even briefly in a Poachyball to subdue it. He made friends with it as if he were another of its kind, and in his second summer back there, he was witness to its first transition into Chickapork. I know how much Hemlock wanted to see the final change to Boarax ... which, sadly, took place in the autumn immediately after Surlymon, so he missed it. This, as I say, was a spiritual quest for him, and he welcomed its transformative intensity from the first, even though in the eyes of other Pokkypet Captors he immediately went from role model to traitor. This was when people started saying he was crazy, sending nasty letters, even making threats. This is when the Missile Kids stepped up their attacks on his character. It got harder and harder for me to bear, but Hemlock said to pay it no mind. It didn't bother him. The only thing that bothered him anymore was any sort of threat to his beloved Pokkypets.

VERNOR HERTZWIG

At the same time that Hemlock Pyne was alienating his former worshippers, he was winning for himself a new audience that would one day be captivated by his insights and his breathtaking cinematic records of his life among the Pokkypets ... a life that few have ever attempted, let alone accomplished. Going through his films, I found him to have possessed an innate genius—not only for capturing Pokkypets, but for capturing moments of pure cinema. Here, we see Pyne in his early summer campsite, a spot he pitched between the dens of burrowing Chickaporks, so that he could live among the frolicking Piglettas.

HEMLOCK PYNE

This is Chickapork. My Chickapork. We're longtime buddies, aren't we, yes we are. Chickapork is my most beloved Pokkypet, and it's really important to understand that we are mutual friends. I do not own him. I did not capture him. I have never imprisoned him in a Poachyball. So you see, it is possible for us to have a harmonious relationship with these beautiful creatures without havinge to ... Hey! This ... this is Pigletta ... this is one of Chickapork's offspring or little sibs, I'm not sure exactly—hey, where are you going with my cap? Come back with that cap, Pigletta! That is a very important cap! That was a gift from Professor Manzanita! Oh ... oh god, oh no.... A lot depends on that cap, Pigletta! Get ... give me back my cap! WHERE'S MY FUCKING POKKYMASTER CAP?

PROFESSOR MANZANITA
POKKYPET EXPERT

In the field, it was obvious that he wanted nothing more than to be a Pokkypet. He would act just like them. The simple continual act of stating his identity with such clarity, this thing the Pokkypets do incessantly, Hemlock adopted this behavior. If you weant out to visit him in the field, or if you were an unsuspecting Captor who came across him, Hem would act as if human language and human behavior were completely unknown to him. He would just say his name at you, over and over, like a Pokkypet. His mantra, his act of affirmation: Hemlock. Hemlock. Hemlock. He saw the Pokky world as a rare and simplified place, everything streamlined and stripped down to this one act of self-naming. That world had a siren's allure for him. But that world ... simply did not exist. The truth was far more complex.

TAIGA MOSS
CURATOR, POKKY NATIONAL WILDERNESS MUSEUM

Well, I'm afraid although Hemlock Pyne might be a hero to some people, to us he seems simply deluded. Our relationship with the Pokkypets goes back tens of thousands of years, to when we believe the Pokkys and people shared this land. We treated each other with respect, and we have done so throughout our history. We created the original Poachyballs, and we captured and collected the first Pokkypets to be captured and collected. We held the first Pokky battles; those rituals are very ancient, the result of the relationship between man and Pokkypet. So there is a very long tradition of understanding between our people and the Pokky people. I would say that what Hemlock did was the ultimate disrespect. In living among the Pokky, in treating them as cute cartoon characters, he crossed a boundary and paid the price. The ultimate price. There is a reason he will not wake up, and honestly, we don't expect him to. I think a lot of people are in denial about the sort of trouble he caused for himself ... and really for all of us, because I don't know if it will stop with Hemlock. There has always been this barrier from time long past ... and he damaged it. Irretrievably. It's plain to see if you'll just look at him. Truly look at him for once.

DR. JASPER CHRYSOLITE
POKKY CLINIC

We are here, in cold storage, at the Pokky Clinic, because quite simply this is the only place we have been able to arrest the very strange and terrible processes that have Hemlock Pyne in their grip. In those steel drawers behind me, if I were to open them, you would see Hemlock Pyne much as he was when they brought him in to me for revival. As you already know, I was unable to wake him, even with the finest waking compounds at my disposal. I say "much as he was" because Hemlock did not stay as he was in those first hours. The separate parts of him lost their normal color ... some began to swell, others to wither ... and there was a terrible odor associated with him, which I would rather not go into. Whatever this process is, some sort of Pokky contagion he caught from Surlymon or elsewhere in the Pokkymaze, I had a sort of hunch that extreme cold might arrest it. And so we arranged for some cold storage, which has indeed seemed to do the trick. We will of course keep trying to wake him as time permits, and if we can devise some other approach to his condition. We also have that Surlymon captive and under observation, in hopes of understanding better what happened ... but for all we can tell, it is simply a Surlymon like every other Surlymon. There is nothing special about it. Which makes us think that whatever strange thing happened to Hemlock Pyne, it was purely a result of his peculiar make-up, his particular situation. It behooves us therefore to try and understand Hemlock himself a little better. Really, what else can we do?

CRYSTAL BURL

Would I say I was his girlfriend? Why, yes, yes I would. I mean, not always, but ... but we were always friends. We founded Pokky People together. We were inseparable. We met when we were both working at Mistress Masham's in the Mall, and Hem was in charge of the Pokky performance. They had a little routine they did where the Pokkys would come out and dance on your table—I mean, various small Pokkys. Nothing large or unhygienic. All the food at Mistress Mashams was served under silver covers, and the Pokkypets would whisk these away with a big flourish. Hem would come out with a half dozen Poachyballs, open them up, and set the Pokkys going. I thought it was pathetic, and I told him so ... and he confided in me that he was only in there as a saboteur. I thought he was kidding, trying to impress me, but no ... one night right after we really got to talking, he went into his usual routine, but everything was different this time. He'd packed a bunch of wild Pokkys into the balls, and he let them loose in the middle of a little kid's birthday party. The Pokkys went crazy—eating up the food, tearing into presents, getting underfoot. And out of nowhere Hem kept producing more and more Poachyballs, opening them up, setting them free. He was laughing, we were both howling, and the more freaked out everybody got, the more delighted Hem was. It seemed to feed the Pokkys' frenzy. They were swinging from the light fixtures, smashing windows, breaking out into the streets ... oh, it was on the news that night and for days, and it was really the beginning of Hem's mystery ... because right after that he disappeared. I didn't see him myself for months and months. It turned out he had made his first visit to the Pokky Range.

VERNOR HERTZWIG

Alone in the wild, Hemlock began to craft his own legend—fashioning himself into a creature as strange and colorful as the Pokkypets he adored. Against a backdrop of untouched wilderness, he portrayed himself an uncivilized man, fearless and ferocious yet as sweet as the creatures he refused to capture. It was as if in liberating the Pokkypets wherever he found them, he was setting free some caged part of himself.

HEMLOCK PYNE

I used to just dabble in Pokkypets. I captured and trained them like everyone else. I saw nothing but what was right in front of me. I never looked any deeper. And I was troubled. Our world, the world of people, is so shallow ... it's just a thin coat of paint, right on the surface, and that's enough for most people. The Pokkys are colorful and cute and uncomplicated, and that's all they need to know. But this wasn't the truth, and without truth I just ... I wasn't making it. I needed the truth that was under all that. I did drugs. I drank. I lived a crazy, crazy life. Nobody knew me. I didn't know myself. I was drinking so much, doing so many drugs, it was destroying my mind. All the colors started to blur together. I couldn't tell Chickapork from Leomonk from Swirlet. It was like when you mix all the colors of paint together and you just get a grayish brownish gunk. And then one day a Flutterflute, I was drinking on the beach, out of my skull, and a Flutterflute landed on the bottle just as I was about to take a swallow. Who knows ... it might have been my last swallow. I might have drained that bottle and thrown it aside and walked out into the waves and that would have been the end. But I watched that Flutterflute there, getting in the way of my drink, and it looked at me and said, "Flutterflute!" That's all, that's what they do. So simple. Just that beautiful simple statement: "Flutterflute." And something in me ... I felt something emerge, as if from a chrysalis, bright and clear and strong, and I said, "Hemlock Pyne." Everything in my life was as simple as that. "Hemlock Pyne." That is what I was, and it was enough. It was deep. And what that meant was everything else was deep. Bottomless. And everything changed for me right then, right that very moment, saying myself back to that Flutterflute. I say it a lot now. It saves me every day: "Hemlock Pyne."

VERNOR HERTZWIG WITH CRYSTAL BURL

VH: Now please explain to the viewers, Crystal, what it is you have here.

CB: What I have here, Vernor, is Hemlock's last recording ... recovered from his campsite ... the recording of the Surlymon.

VH: Now I understand there is some uncertainty whether the recorder was running already or whether it was turned on during the Surlymon's attack, and if so whether it was Hemlock himself or the Surlymon that switched it on. But that doesn't really matter, does it? What matters is the contents of the tape, which you, I believe, have never listened to, is that correct?

CB: That is correct. Dr. Chrysolite said I had probably better not.

VH: Dr. Chrysolite is a wise man and you do well to listen to him, but his prohibition does not apply to me, so I am going to listen to the recording now. The lens cap was never removed during the battle, I am just going to listen to the recording if I have your permission to do so.

CB: I give it, yes.

VH: If you will, please, to start the ... there now, I hear wind, very loud, and something like a ripping sound ... perhaps the tent's zipper. Actually, yes, it sounds as if the Surlymon is coming in range. I can hear it quite clearly saying its name over and over again: Surlymon ... Surlymon.... And now clearly I hear Hemlock, much closer. Of course we know he had no Poachyballs, and no other Pokkys with him at the time. He is really alone against this creature. The Surlymon is saying again, "Surlymon. Surlymon." And occasionally just "Surly," as if it is too excited to say its full name.

CB: They do that sometimes when they're excited ... even add extra syllables....

VH: And now Pyne is ... he seems to have hit on a desperate strategy ... he is saying his own name several times to the creature. It is almost as if they are having a conversation, like so: Surly ... Surlymon ... and Hemlock says Hemlock. Hemlock Pyne. Hemlock. He's saying it again. And the Surlymon seems to be having none of it. Surlymon. Hemlock Pyne. Surlymon. Surlymon. Hemlock Pyne. Hemlock Pyne. Hemlock. Surlymon. And now a terrible, terrible sound. You ... you must never listen to this recording, Crystal.

CB: That's what Dr. Chrysolite recommended as well, Vernor.

VH: Hemlock Pyne. Hemlock Pyne. Hemlock ... Surlymon. And now I hear nothing but Surlymon. You must destroy this tape, Crystal. I think that is the only course of action.

CB: I will, Vernor. I will.

VH: Surly. Surlymon. Surlymon. Surly.

HEMLOCK PYNE

We are here at the edge of the Pokkypet Arena, deep in the Pokkymaze. The Pokkys have never allowed me this close before, but I think it is a sign of their acceptance—a sign of how far I've come—that they are allowing me to set up my camera here overlooking the arena and film their battles in progress. Remember, these are entirely natural and unstaged ... these are not like the Coliseum battles that human captors arrange, which go against the will and the inherent nature of the Pokkypets. What you are seeing here is the source of humanity's watered-down commercially driven arena battles. This, my friends, is the real shit.

Now it looks like a Scanary is going into the arena, setting the first challenge.... Scanaries have three attacks: Wing Blast, Chirplosion, and Tauntalon. This is a fairly good combination unless your Pokkynemesis happens to have natural resistance to more than one of these. Let's keep our fingers crossed. And now ... it looks like ... yes, it's a Pyrovulp. Oh, this is going to be intense! Pyrovulps are extremely vulnerable to Tauntalon—extremely. But if the little guy can get past the Scanary's first attack, then things could get interesting. And it looks like ... Scanary is rearing back, puffing up a little bit ... just look at those gorgeous chest feathers ... could be Tauntalon coming in first.... But no! Wings going out, we've got a blast coming in, and Pyrovulp has got its head flame forward. This was a very bad move on Scanary's part, and I think it's going to regret.... Would you look at that! Wing Blast has fed Pyrovulp's headflame. The whole Pokky is on fire, just burning up ... this lets Pyrovulp bypass an entire part of its normal attack and go straight to Auraflame! The only risk, and I'm not sure he knows it, is that Auraflame can easily feed into Scanary's own ... oh my god oh my god.... Auraflame, incredibly powerful and hot, has triggered Scanary's innate Chirplosion. I am moving away from the Arena, friends, because when this happens, the blast can spread far outside the—WHOA!

VERNOR HERTZWIG

In his records, Hemlock speaks less and less of the human world; civilization and its pleasures recede into the distant past, remembered only for its discontents. At the same time, the brilliant, colorful struggles of the Pokkypets, seeming so much simpler, become more and more a symbol for the conflict of his soul. Deeply torn, it is as if he battled himself in an arena of his own devising. But no longer a Captor or a Trainer, without Pokkypets to do his fighting for him, every injury cut deep into his psyche.

LARCHMONT AND GLADIOLUS PYNE
HEMLOCK'S PARENTS

LP: This is Hem's Pokkypet collection, much as he left it when he moved away from home. I'm afraid we encouraged him more than we should have, since he was a somewhat lonely boy, and he got such pleasure from them. His first Pokkypet was a gift from my mother, who had an affinity herself with the little things—

GP: I thought he won it at a state fair, throwing dimes in Collymoddle bowls, or a prize he won at school.

LP: —no, it was from my mother. I think he's still got the card in his room somewhere pinned up on a bulletin board. We knew there wasn't much of a future in it, but that's not the sort of thing you can worry about when you just want your boy to be happy ... but as he got older and we saw he wasn't moving on to other things, wasn't progressing if you will, then we started to get a bit worried. But somehow Hemlock found a way to make a living at it early on, doing his shows and trainings and whatnot; and although we were disappointed that he felt he had to move all the way to the other side of the country to pursue his interests, we did support him in it. It seemed like his Pokky career was really taking him somewhere. Then, well, I don't know how much truth there is in this, but he tried out for the part of Burny, the Pokky Trainer in Chirrs, and according to him he was first in line for the part, but then Woody Harrelson tried out for the role and they gave it to him. Well, really, that was the beginning of the end for our boy.

GP: He just sort of spiralled out of control.

LP: I held it against Woody for a long time, but ... well....

GP: It's hard to keep a grudge against Woody Harrelson. He's a fine young man.

CRYSTAL BURL

We used to go to the Pokkypet stores in the mall, and Hem would get really upset looking at them in captivity, and he always talked about starting a Pokkypet Liberation Front—but that's not what Pokky People is about or ever was about. Pokky People allowed him to channel his frustration into something positive. You have to understand, the frustration turned so easily into anger. He could be the happiest most joyful person you'd ever met, but the flipside of that was ... was also there. He could be very dark at times. I know he felt that if he didn't have Pokkys, he'd have gone to some very bad places with some very bad people. The Missile Kids, for instance—they tried to recruit him for a while, and I think he was attracted. They could be very seductive. You know, Minny was a real minx, and Sal was sarcastic and cutting, but I know Hem respected them as Trainers ... and then that weird Pokky they had with them all the time, Feelion. In the way that Hem could almost convince the Pokkys that he was one of them, Feelion had a bunch of us convinced that he was one of us. But though Hem flirted with the Missile Kids, he eventually came to believe they were on a bad path—I mean, certainly in terms of drugs they were doing crazy things ... I think even their Pokky was on amphetamines.

HEMLOCK PYNE

If people knew, truly knew what wonderful creatures these Pokkypets are ... they would consider, as I do, that to capture them, to try and train them, to force them through their tri-stage transformations at an accelerated pace—that all this goes against nature. Look at little Chickapork here ... just look at her. She is my hero. So sweet, so loving, so intelligent ... truly a hero. And to think that people want to put her in a ball and give her performance drugs and and and just dump her out in the coliseum to battle against other Pokkys that humans—fucking humans!—have declared her enemies ... it's just sick! And it makes me so angry. Because she's perfect. The lifestyle they live out here in the wild, it's perfect. I have learned so much from these creatures, but it's hardly the beginning of what we could all be learning from them. Our lives ... there's something missing from them that these Pokkys have mastered effortlessly. We need that thing. We don't even know what we're missing ... but I'll tell you ... it's something fucking huge. And without it, we're so far short of perfection it's not funny. That's why nobody's laughing, isn't that right, little Chickapork?

VERNOR HERTZWIG

As his differences with reality widened into a schism, Hemlock Pyne fought reality with tooth and claw. If it did not fit his idealized view of nature, it was reality that must be bent and even broken to fit. His insistence that Pokkypets held a deeper meaning does not stand up to scrutiny. Where Hemlock looked at the colorful characters and saw inscrutable depths, I see only crisp lines, primary colors, two-dimensional expressions. Even in this Rhinophantom, which Pyne in his writings calls a juggernaut of disaster, evokes in me no such premonition. It is just a cute, cuddly pet, that has undergone completely ordinary metamorphoses into a brute that is dumb and awkward, yes, but completely without malice.

HEMLOCK PYNE

...What I found in the bushes here, by the side of the river, is something new to the Pokkymaze. I would like you to study it with me. This is something we have to understand, but I'm not convinced we can. We are so good at missing the point! I discovered this earlier today, just after dawn, and I haven't touched the scene ... I've just been waiting for it to get light enough to record. Now, in the night there was the sound of a Pokkybattle. This is rare enough, but not unheard of in midsummer. What is unusual is that it took place far from the Arena, and quite near my tent. Just a very weird sound of two Pokkys calling back and forth to one another in solitary combat. I couldn't hear them clearly, but you can see now that they both cast exhausting spells on one another, and, well, here they are. They show no signs of waking or getting along with their day. You can see the Porphyrops has been trampled down into the mud, and the Glumster is just lying with its eyes open, which is a strange position for an incapacitated Pokky. I don't want to intrude in their natural cycle, but I've made some very gentle sounds and I've been getting progressively louder, trying to see if I can wake them gradually. But so far no luck. I have to say, I feel very privileged to see this. To my knowledge no Pokky Captor or Trainer has ever observed this sort of behavior. I am the first. These are the sort of secret revelations the Pokkys have granted me now that I have become such a part of their pattern of life. And these are exactly the things that I need to protect from the rest of the world.

AUGUSTUS "JUSTICE" PEACE

There were really no poachers in this area. The one exception might be the Missile Kids, Sal and Minny, and their Pokky mascot Feelion. But I don't believe they went up there to poach anyhow. The couple times we were concerned and apprehended them, there was no sign they'd been up to any actual Pokkypoaching. What they did do, I'm pretty certain, was show up to bother Hemlock Pyne. Tease him. They made a lot out of being his rivals, you know. And I'm sure it drove him nuts.

HEMLOCK PYNE

I'm here at the shore, this is so upsetting, here at the shore watching those fuckers ... those goddamn poachers ... Sal and Minny. I know what they're up to. They're rubbing my nose in it, that's what they're doing. They've come in to poach—look at that boat full of Poachyballs! There's just no question ... they know I'm watching even though I'm well hidden here. What kills me, fucking KILLS me, is that they have the full support of the Pokky Park Service. It's criminal. It's so corrupt! You just ... the lesson here is that you just pay off the right people and you can come in and capture all the Pokkypets you want. Well, I'm not letting them get away with it. They think they can ... what's that?

"Feeeeee-lion!"

Do you you hear that? They've turned their Feelion loose.

"FEEEEE-LION!"

This is just sick, it's perverted. They've trained their Pokkypet to turn against its kind. This poor Feelion doesn't realize they're using it to lure in unsuspecting Pokkypets ... to pull them in where the Missile Kids can capture them. Well, we're not going to let them get away with that. No fucking way.

"Can you Feeeeel me, Pyne? Can you Feeeeeeeelion me?"

Did you hear that? So much for them calling me paranoid. There's no mistaking that for ... for a threat!

"Feeeeee-lion!"

The cruel thing is, I can't even report them. Because I know they are here with the full knowledge of the Park Service. I can't believe I get grief for coming out here to protect these poor creatures, while Minny and Sal just waltz in, pack their Poachyballs full of innocent, defenseless Pokkys.... To think the rangers would actually try to stop me from getting close to the pets, while these guys ... I'm sorry, I can't talk. This is making me too upset. I'm in tears over this!

VERNOR HERTZWIG

Pyne's disgruntlement became so great that he finally turned against the people who had given him the opportunity to work in the Pokkymaze in the first place. His associates became, in his mind, implacable enemies. There is a sense in his final days of rage that he no longer saw anything beyond the picket of Pokkys, among whom he counted himself, except an homogenous foe.

HEMLOCK PYNE

Oh, I know who they are, all right ... I know they set me up for this those ... those goddamn fucking motherfuckers. You know who you are, you fucking shithead mothercockingfucksuckfuckers! I'm out here trying to help these beautiful creatures, while you're just swimming in corruption ... you don't care a thing about preserving their environment. You people who have sworn to protect it, you've become the thing we have to protect it against! Motherfuck! This ... it's just not right. It's fucked. So very, very, very, very fucked.

CRYSTAL BURL, AUGUSTUS "GUST" MASTERS, PITER YALP

We've come here today to honor Hem, and to pray for him to wake up real soon. We don't understand what happened to him—what was different this time that he refuses to wake up. We were thinking that maybe if we came out here, to a place that was dear to him, we'd have some insight ... we'd get a glimpse of Hem's thinking.

This right here is his favorite camping spot, where he'd come and spend the first part of the summer at the foot of the Pokky Range before heading north into the Maze. He chose this spot because it was right between two Chickapork dens. There's footage of him playing with the Piglettas, and then of course when one of them made its second-stage transformation into Chickapork, Hem and that Pokky bonded real hard. It's been a year now, and those original Pokkys have gone on and become Peccanaries and Boaraxes; the ones grazing out there in the meadow, one of them might have been Hem's own Chickapork.

I wonder if they miss him. I sure do.

VERNOR HERTZWIG

The irony of Hemlock's last trip is not lost on anyone who looked at his life. As the days of fall grew shorter, he left the maze as he always did, with no desire to return to civilization, but knowing he could not make himself comfortable among the hibernating and overwintering Pokkys. However, an encounter with an airport Pokkypet vending machine, in which Hemlock tried to buy the freedom of every captive Pokkypet but soon ran out of quarters, sent him rebounding from the crass commercial exploitation of his beloved Pokkys, straight back into the wilderness. Returning to the maze later than ever before, he found his familiar environment had been altered by advancing chill; and his familiar Pokky friends had moved on their migratory routes, while new creatures moved into the maze to overwinter there. Creatures such as the Surlymon.

HEMLOCK PYNE

I am back, friends. I didn't know I would be doing this, obviously, and I would not recommend it to anyone else ... but frankly, I find it exhilarating. I am overjoyed to be back here. The longer I can put off dealing with the fucking human world, the happier I'll be. And you know what? This is a part of the Pokky life cycle I have never seen. This is a learning moment! I have never been here in the winter ... and though I won't be staying for the whole season, I will certainly see more of it than any person ever has. Because no other person—Trainer, Captor, or civilian—has stayed even this long. Who knows what I'll learn, what wonders await?

VERNOR HERTZWIG

Toward the end of the process of compiling this account, we received access to Pyne's final recordings. Here we see him with a large grouchy Pokkypet that almost certainly is the Surlymon that finished him off. Of most interest in these studies is that this Pokky appears to have changed radically sometime between the date this footage was taken, and the time of its capture by the Pokky Rangers. Experience gained in a battle is the usual mode by which Pokkys gain sufficient energy to transform into their morpheme. And it is hard not to conclude that it was the battle with Hemlock Pyne that caused this Surlymon to undergo its third transformation. Most confusing to Pokkyologists is that while its form changed dramatically, its name and its song remained the same: Surlymon....

Here, Hemlock records the untransformed Surlymon stalking the maze in an endless search for amusement. He seems to be searching this simple creature for a deeper meaning, but whatever it is eludes him, as it eludes us.

HEMLOCK PYNE

I don't know what this Pokky wants. Superficially, it seems to be looking for food and interested in nothing else. But there is something the Pokkys have, something innate in them, which draws me. I feel sometimes so close to them, I almost have a name for it—one I could express to myself, but which might be impossible to communicate to others. There is something ... something there.

VERNOR HERTZWIG

But here I must disagree with Hemlock Pyne. The cute cartoon features, so simplistic and round and bright, need evoke nothing beyond the simplest emotional connotations associated with their coloration. He looks for depth where none exists. The Pokkys have no secrets, and nothing to teach us. If anything, this is their entire lesson: They mean nothing, and nothing about their relationship with us is real.

DR. JASPER CHRYSOLITE

If I open this door and pull out the tray, you can see the desperate effort we have undertaken to keep Hemlock comfortable in spite of the bizarre process that seems to be having its way with him. Here you see his head, the eyes still closed in an attitude of sleep that for all intents and purposes seems permanent. Here, his hand, somewhat distressed after its short stay in Surlymon's mouth. The torso, on which the head hardly fits at this point. Part of a leg. The other parts, all gathered from the maze, do not quite add up completely. But this still seems the sort of risk Hemlock stated repeatedly he was willing to take to be one with these creatures, to learn the lessons they carried with them. Lessons, perhaps, that may one day apply to us, as we share their natural world?

HEMLOCK PYNE

I know I have felt something like this before, but the shortness of the season sharpens this sense of giving. I have the words now. They have given them to me. I owe the Pokkypets everything I have. Everything. And I owe them completely. I would die for these creatures. I would die for these creatures. I would die for these creatures.

VERNOR HERTZWIG

We still have no idea what he means.

Author Comments

Rick Hautala

"I always thought I would have fit right into the literary scene in Concord, Massachusetts, in the 1840s ... You know, when Hawthorne, Thoreau, Emerson, and the Alcotts were kicking around. Of all the folks in Concord, I believe Bronson Alcott and I would have seen eye-to-eye on most things, so I was only too happy to rework Louisa May Alcott's *Little Women*. I'd like to think Louisa and her father would get a kick out of what I did to her story ... I hope so, anyway. Otherwise, there will be hell to pay in the literary afterlife."

Rick Hautala's most recent short story collection is *Occasional Demons*, from CD Publications, and he's finishing up a novella titled *Indian Summer*.

Marc Laidlaw

"Odd juxtapositions are rocket fuel for a writer's imagination. One inadvertent swap of unrelated concepts, one irresistible pun, may give instantaneous rise to an entire universe. Thus it was with 'Pokky Man,' which emerged full-blown from the title—a vision of filmmaker Werner Herzog trapped in a shallow cartoon world he would certainly consider unworthy of his time and energy. This cartoon world was inspired by a popular kids' videogame, especially the version where you're a nature photographer, drifting through a dynamic yet unchanging landscape of cartoon creatures fixed in Dantesque tableaux."

Marc Laidlaw, writer of the popular Half-Life series of videogames, is currently at work on several secret projects at Valve Software.

Tom Piccirilli

"I always wanted to do a dark fantasy tale focusing on a Mafioso hitman running across witches. It seemed a natural match-up: all those bad guys who used to be altar boys, plied with Catholic doctrine and surrounded by priests and nuns and old country iconography. I figured if a hitman ever did run into the supernatural he'd probably be ready for it, having been raised with all that heavy, spooky symbolism. Add to it the naughty draw of a sex symbol like Jayne Mansfield and you've got enough Catholic guilt to fuel a guns blazing novella."

Tom Piccirilli's latest crime novel is *The Last Kind Words* from Bantam Books.

Lezli Robyn

"When I was a pre-teen I was given the L. M. Montgomery books for Christmas. It was my first introduction to her most famous character, Anne Shirley, and I was hooked. Like me, Anne wanted to be a writer, and she had such a zest for life; such an infectious imagination. I jumped at the chance to write an Anne story for this mashup collection, mixing the classic story of a young orphan girl proving her worth and finding a place to belong, with the popular Steampunk genre. Thus, 'Anne-droid of Green Gables' was born."

Lezli Robyn is an Australian writer who has been nominated for the 2010 Campbell and Aurealis awards, and has story collection coming from Ticonderoga Publications in 2012. "Anne-droid of Green Gables" has also been selected for the 2011's *Year's Best Australian Fantasy and Horror* anthology.

Tom Tessier

"Senator Joseph McCarthy was a fascinating figure in postwar American history, cartoonish and laughable but also dangerous and destructive. He was a master at creating fear in the public mind and then using it for his own purposes. I couldn't resist putting him in a classic horror situation and seeing what would happen. McCarthy is long dead, but McCarthyism, sad to say, is still very much alive in the land."

Thomas Tessier is working on a new novel, *The Lives of the Banshee*.

Editor Comment

Jeff Conner

"It was a real pleasure to work with the writers on this collection. Each one brought a fresh perspective to what some refer to as Monster Lit, altering the landscape as they explored new and fresh possibilities. I believe that the 3R books go way beyond shallow formulas, which is why we call our version of mash-up fiction 'CTL-ALT-Lit.' Here at IDW we do far more than simply insert a genre-flavored filling into a bland Twinkie of public domain literature or historical icons. So don't eat that—*eat this*!"

Jeff Conner is a practicing editor who currently heads up IDW's line of original prose projects. Along with the three volumes of RRR, he recently worked on *GI JOE: Tales From The Cobra Wars*, a collection of original fiction set in the same world as IDW's *G.I. JOE* comics. He is a World Fantasy Award recipient and has written three non-fiction media tie-in books.